The Reconstructionist

BY THE SAME AUTHOR

Damage
Sin
Oblivion
The Stillest Day

The Reconstructionist

Josephine Hart

THE OVERLOOK PRESS
Woodstock & New York

First published in paperback in the United States by
The Overlook Press, Peter Mayer Publishers, Inc.
Woodstock & New York

WOODSTOCK:
One Overlook Drive
Woodstock, NY 12498
www.overlookpress.com
[for individual orders, bulk and special sales contact our Woodstock office]

NEW YORK:
141 Wooster Street
New York, NY 10012

Library of Congress Cataloging-in-Publication Data
Hart, Josephine
The reconstructionist / Josephine Hart.
p. cm.
1. Brothers and sisters—Fiction.   2. London (England) Fiction.
3. Psychiatrists—Fiction.   4. Divorced men—Fiction.   5. Ireland—Fiction.   I. Title

Manufactured in the United States of America
ISBN 1-58567-322-6
1 3 5 7 9 8 6 4 2

FOR M. AND THE BOYS

On this third planet of the sun
among the signs of bestiality
a clear conscience is Number One.

Wisława Szymborska

Afterwards

———

. . . WE WERE asked to reconstruct the event. Much detail was required of us concerning how the hours had been spent between midday, when we had been seen to return from church, and four-thirty that afternoon when they broke the window and entered the house. A moment I see now as the first moment of dispossession.

They found us sitting on high-backed chairs, placed exactly opposite each other in the stone hallway. It was a position from which we had not moved for over an hour. We were obedient children. That day we did exactly as our father had ordered before he silently, and for the last time, left the house.

Later, and with those who loved us, we too departed. Or, more accurately, we were removed as though we were precious objects, which must be saved at all costs from the inferno. Removal from the house in which we had spent our childhood was not, however, deemed adequate protection. We were transported, therefore, again by those who loved us, to another country.

And as the doors of that old life closed behind us, others opened. We were guided through a corridor of time designed to take us far away from that Sunday in August and from the house in which the event took place. We were encouraged into a life which would, in its busy intensity, lay siege to memory and, it was hoped, finally kill it.

The years moved us down the river and we dipped our oars lightly. Nature had created me an observer and I had inherited from someone, not my parents, a cool mind. She had been fashioned in another mode. She had inherited from them not only beauty but also something striking in her colouring which made her unforgettable. She could not have ignored this inheritance, even if she'd wanted to. So strong was its impact that a privileged education – St. Paul's, followed by Cambridge – became not the driving force to a life of achievement, but simply another adornment and, over time, the least important.

My own achievement in life, such as it is, is due in part to the judicious application of the knowledge I gained through years of study and training. It is due also to the almost obsessive attention that I pay to the body language, tone of voice and expression in the eyes of almost everyone with whom I come into close contact. Professionally, I have no doubt this has been of enormous advantage to me. Personally, this alert and constant vigilance is practised in the hope that, in discerning, even in the distance, a shadowy outline of potential danger, I may be able to pre-empt it.

I am a very busy man. I make this statement, as other busy men do, with rueful pride. Like them, I am in fact grateful for my demanding, professional life. Its daily pressures – and pressure, of course, gives balance – provide an antidote to the potentially fatal seduction of memory. Perversely, however, my hours are spent in investigation of the memories of others.

One

‌

Today, Friday, this afternoon to be precise, I am informed by her current husband, Ian, that my first wife, Ellie, has had a heart attack.

"Jack?"

"Yes . . ."

"It's Ian."

"Yes?" My tone is wary. I wonder if he notices.

"Look, Ellie's ill."

"Oh, God, I'm so sorry." It must be serious; otherwise he wouldn't ring me.

"Thanks, Jack. As you can imagine, it's a terrible shock."

"What is it? I mean . . . what happened?"

"Heart attack. It's minor, thank God. To tell you the truth, I'm stunned. I mean . . . she's normally so healthy. It's such a pity. She was thrilled they'd been invited to do a short European tour of *L'Héritage*. You know . . . the Maupassant adaptation she won that prize for. God, I'm so upset I can't even remember what it was."

"The *Prix Jean Vilar*?" It's pathetic of me, particularly in these circumstances, to feel a sense of one-upmanship, but I do.

"Yes, that's it! Anyway, they'd just arrived in Paris. It was her first tour abroad since the children were born. She's concentrated more on radio and TV over the last few years. But when she won this prize, we had a little talk about it – round-table confab – you know the sort of thing. I knew the children would miss her dreadfully, but I explained to them that it was such a great opportunity Mummy couldn't let this chance pass."

I resist the urge to analyse any aspect of Ian's version of the sad history of the flight of the mother from her distraught babes.

"She's brilliant, you know," he continues.

Who does he think he's talking to? An acquaintance of Ellie's? I found her, you stupid man . . .

"And then, of course, there's the languages. Remember?"

"Yes, Ian, I remember the languages."

I try to communicate my irritation by sighing, but it's wasted on him. Still, it's true. I, too, had been dazzled by "the languages". Fluent French, German, Italian. Smattering of Greek. And, this was the killer line, "adequate Spanish". Wrap that up in a man's trench coat, weird little boots and an out-of-date pony-tail held in a rubber band, add driving artistic ambition and, well, I married her. Who wouldn't?

"I'd really like to get to Paris tonight. And, Jack, the ghastly thing is, Ellie's mother is in America with Richard and you won't believe this, but the nanny's in hospital. Emergency appendicitis. It's half-term and most of our friends have gone away. I know it's a lot to ask, Jack, but can you take them till Rose arrives? She's trying to get a flight from Minneapolis to New York and on to London. Where exactly is Minneapolis, Jack?"

"It's in the Midwest."

"Oh, well . . . Jack, do you think you can help out?"

Domestic imperatives and crises at which, Ellie, you were always hopeless. And though you are ill, Ellie, all I can think is, doesn't he have anyone else? Followed by, why the hell is he doing this to me? I know we had a civilized divorce, but this is ridiculous. Anyway, I barely know your children. Are you really very ill, Ellie? Can this be true?

"Jack? Are you still there?"

"Yes, Ian. I'm still here. And yes, of course, I can take them."

"Oh, thanks, thanks. God, that's a relief. Can I drop them off on my way to the airport? Say in just over an hour?"

"Yes, that's fine. I've just got back from the hospital and I've got one late appointment here. But by the time you arrive, I'll be free. I'll ask Kate to come and help."

A pause.

"Kate?"

"Yes, Kate. My sister, Kate. You remember."

"We never met," Ian says, rather coolly.

Which is a bit of a nerve, considering. And I remember that Ellie had never liked Kate. Had rather despised her, in a way.

"OK, Jack. If you think it's a good idea. They're being very good about it, the children. I haven't told them everything, of course. Just that Mummy's sick in Paris. They know it's reasonably serious, otherwise I wouldn't leave them. I don't think they really believe it's happening. You must come across that a lot, Jack. Disbelief. You'll know what to say."

"I'll do my best, Ian."

God, this is madness. The suddenness of all this has made me forget the names of the children. Those children . . .

"Margaret's nearly eight now, and Harry's six. It's a

while since you've seen them. I'll be around in about an hour and a half. Is that OK?"

"Fine. And Ian, I'm so sorry."

I can't say send my love to Ellie. Or can I? Before I have a chance to say anything . . .

"Thanks, Jack. I'll give Ellie your love. And Jack, I can't thank you enough. Right, I'd better pack a few things for them."

"OK. See you."

As I put the phone down, the doorbell rings. I press the entry system and Sir George Bywater pounds up the stairs, strides into the room and, sighing loudly, throws himself into the chair opposite mine. It is a high-backed, revolving, green leather chair. It has been placed at a particular angle to my own, which is, and this is important to me, non-revolving. Sir George Bywater glares at me and begins to speak.

"It was a disaster. A complete, fucking disaster. Sorry. Sorry. I've been trying to control myself since we got back on Sunday night. God, I wish I'd been able to come on Wednesday. But it's been a hellish week. One crucial meeting after another. And then our AGM yesterday. Which was tough, let me tell you. My God, some of these analysts! Twenty-three, twenty-four years of age and they think they know it all! So I couldn't let go. I've had to stay in complete control. Oh, God. Oh, my God. I'm going to cry . . . Jesus! Why don't you say something?"

"You say it."

"I need new friends. I've got to get new friends. I need a new life. They look at me and they see her standing beside me. I don't think I can pull it off. I really don't think I can. I can see them thinking of her. Comparing . . ."

"What makes you so certain of that?"

"You think I'm wrong?" The note in his voice is hopeful.

"I think it's possible. It's at least possible. They're not thinking of . . ."

I glance at his notes, which thankfully he doesn't seem to notice.

". . . Alice, but of Trisha."

"Patricia! We've agreed Patricia."

"Ah . . ."

"Yes. I mentioned it to her this weekend. She was a bit taken aback but she agreed. Frankly, it was the only thing that went right the entire weekend."

"Was it important to you to call her Patricia, rather than Trisha? You think it sounds better?"

"Christ, I've embarrassed myself enough in front of you. Yes, I think it sounds better. It's because I'm slightly ashamed of her. There! I've said it."

"Are you sure that's the reason?"

"Yes, I'm sure. I know I'm pathetic. It's pathetic at my age to need the approval of my circle."

"What does Trisha . . . Patricia's . . . circle, think of you?"

"Her circle? I haven't met her circle. I doubt she has one. She's a single woman of a certain age. She wants to be taken over, to use my terminology. Her allegiances are therefore weaker. She's in transit at the moment. She hasn't arrived. That sounds brutal, I know."

"And you, and your circle, have arrived?"

"I've no illusions. My circle is an interdependent grouping of disparate entities which, over the years, has coalesced into a great marketing force."

"That's quite a description."

"It's from my company report. We went through it this

morning. The phrase lodged."

"Why do you think Tri——"

"Patricia . . ."

"The issue of names may have more to do with your desire to test her, to ask for a sacrifice, than with some kind of latent . . ."

". . . Snobbery? Maybe you're right. Alice wouldn't have liked her."

"Why not?"

"Alice was a . . ."

". . . A snob?"

"Yes. Yes, she was. Don't get me wrong. She was a lovely woman. But yes, she was a snob. Family, not money. She despised money."

"Of which you've made rather a lot."

"Yes, it's ridiculous. I mean, by American standards I'm a pauper, an absolute pauper. But by English standards I've made a lot of money. In Alice's terms, a vulgar amount of money. When I sold Canning Industries she was mortified. Totally mortified. The papers were full of the price I got for my shareholding. She hated the publicity. She was terrified of ostentation. Her father's an academic, a left-wing hereditary peer. Didn't like me much. Likes me less now. Though he's very old. Do you think the old hate less? The way they say they love less? Anyway, he's got reason to hate me, as you can imagine."

I can indeed. But I rather like Sir George – this flailing captain of industry, as he sits opposite me in my uncluttered room. A tired and confused man of a certain age; uncertain of what, if anything, age should determine in his life.

"Though you know," he goes on, "Alice wasn't his

favourite child, not even favourite daughter. No, he worshipped Binkie."

"Binkie?"

"Alice's youngest sister. She's rather marvellous. Lives in South Africa now. In Johannesburg. Amazing she's ended up in the murder capital of the world! He worries about her all the time. She's forty-seven and he's still worrying about her. At the moment, I'm not so much worried about my own children, as bloody furious with them."

"Yes. We talked about it last week."

"Well, it's worse now. I mean, they're not just being difficult. They're being impossible. Totally bloody impossible. That's what I said to my brother, Charles, the other day. We were having our regular monthly lunch at the Savoy. And Charles looked away from me, embarrassed, and started playing with his food like some goddamn model on a diet. Then he put his fork down in this very deliberate way, looked straight at me and said, 'They're not being difficult, George. They're not being difficult. They're grieving. They're in mourning.' 'My God, Charles,' I said, 'you sound like one of those trauma counsellors.' Sorry. I mean, well, they're different. Not as well-trained as you – obviously."

In his delightful way, Sir George has more or less dismissed my medical qualification, my time at the Maudsley, not to mention my years in practice. Something about him makes me find this amusing, rather than insulting.

". . . Anyway, my children are in their twenties. My eldest son is nearly thirty, for God's sake. I'd understand if they were small, or even teenagers. But thirty? Couldn't they just let me get on with my life? I mean, it's so unfair."

"Have you considered the possibility that your brother – Charles, is it? – that he's right? That they *are* in mourning?"

"But it's over a year! They can't still be in mourning. I know what they want. They want me to stay there – at a kind of full stop. I'm to be the keeper, the keeper of the flame, as far as their mother is concerned. You know, sometimes I hate them. I really hate them. I'm sorry. I just have to say it. I hate my children. Well, what do you say?"

"It's not uncommon. Particularly in this situation."

"Well, it's a hell of a shock to me. You may be used to this. But, Christ, how can I hate them so much? All right, you told me last time: guilt. It's a bit of a fucking cliché. I'm not guilty. My God, anyone would think I'd murdered my wife. She died from an illness. NOT MY FAULT. That's what I want to scream at them. It's not my fault."

"They know that."

"Well, you wouldn't think it from their behaviour. They've only met Patricia once and it was absolutely ghastly. Now they simply refuse to see her at all. I'm frightened that she'll be put off, you know, by their hostility. I took them out to dinner before the weekend, that disastrous weekend, to Harry's Bar. Do you have any idea of the expense? Four grown-up children and their spouses and partners. What the hell is a partner, may I ask you? I've got partners but I don't want to live with them. I don't want to live with a partner. I want a wife . . ."

". . . Another wife. That's how your children see it, I would guess."

"Yes, all right. Another wife. I want Patricia. I want her. They're not going to stop me."

"They can't."

"Oh, can't they? Have you ever been patronized by your over-educated, pompous children who believe in every politically correct cliché in the book – except when it comes to their father? They're bloody conservative then, I can tell you. Do you know what children want? I'll tell you. They want surrender. They want total fucking surrender. They want unconditional surrender. And they're not magnanimous in victory, either. Oh no."

"But they're parents themselves. You told me last time we talked."

"Well, two of them are. My eldest son, Andrew, has a little boy, Peter, a year old, and Sophie's just had a baby girl, Jessica. Both born after . . . after Alice. They haven't a clue about it. They think they're parents because they have babies. It's all just physical now. Kissing them. Feeding them. They haven't a clue. I had a tough time with my father. Much tougher than they've had with me. Tell me, does anyone come to you and complain of the mess their grandparents made of bringing up their parents? I doubt it. No, the poor old parents take the hit for the whole goddamn thing. Oh God, I'm going to cry again. Oh fuck, is it often like this? Crying at the beginning and at the end?"

"In a way, it's always like that. In a way."

"Do you ever think about me when I'm not here?"

"I look at your notes. Tell me a little about the weekend."

"Oh, I suppose it wasn't too terrible. I feel calmer now. I've just been so tense about this weekend. It's been looming over me for months. You see, we – well, Alice and I – we always went to Tom Aronson's mother's house in Menton, just outside Monte Carlo, for the

Grand Prix. I was at school with Tom. He was mad about racing and so was I and it became a kind of tradition, I suppose. Then Adrian Barlow joined us one year and we've been meeting there ever since. Even when Tom spent four years in New York, he always made it back for the Grand Prix. In the beginning we didn't take wives or girlfriends, but that changed when Tom married an American and she insisted, you know the way they do. God, they're stubborn, women! Well, she was right. It worked. The girls went shopping and we went to the circuit.

"A few months ago, somehow, stupidly, I told Patricia about Menton and she kind of looked at me and said nothing for a minute. Which unnerved me. Silence does, you see. So I kind of rushed in and said – would you like to come? The minute, I mean, the very minute I said it, I cursed myself. I prayed she'd say no, it's too early. But she just smiled and said, I'd love to. Absolutely love to. Oh God! I had to write an excruciating letter to Tom and his mother, she's pure poison, I can tell you. Anyway, I was trapped. Menton it was, with Patricia.

"Christ, I was nervous. I nearly crashed the car on the drive from Nice. I was constantly looking over at her thinking what the hell will they make of her? What will they think of her after . . . Alice? I kept checking her clothes. She was wearing a grey trouser suit and when she took the jacket off, I actually wondered if her cream blouse was Chanel. Alice always told me they make the best silk blouses. That's what you learn in a long marriage. Little gems like that. And Alice loved clothes. It was the one thing about my money which she really enjoyed.

"Then I saw the sandals! She was wearing green, strappy, high-heeled sandals. I hadn't noticed them on the plane. Maybe she changed her shoes while I was collecting the car, I don't know. And I said to her, trying to sound casual, do you think they're suitable? And she said, what? Do I think what's suitable? And I nodded down at the sandals. She didn't get angry or anything. She just gave me that enigmatic smile of hers and said, oh, I think they're perfectly suitable, George. It's a beautiful day in the South of France and they only have a tiny heel. And George, I'm fully aware, because you told me, my dear, that Alice always, always wore Ferragamo pumps during the day, leather or patent. Or even canvas in the summer, if she wanted to be truly casual.

"And you know what . . . I suddenly wanted to cry, about Alice and that neat little row of Ferragamo pumps, immaculate little things. I thought what an innocent pleasure it had been for her. And then I thought, no more Ferragamo, Alice. And I wondered, if I married Patricia, what would I see when I looked down at her shoe rail? I got so upset thinking about those little shoes that I almost turned round there and then. But I didn't. Which even I know meant a lot. It meant Patricia could mock, gently – I'm not saying she was mean or anything – but Patricia could mock Alice and her little shoes, and I'd let her.

"Then I thought, let's be positive here, you know, look at Patricia's good points. That's what I always do in a crisis, think positive. But all that came to mind was, at least she's not twenty-something. Can you imagine the ridicule? Patricia's thirty-four. Oh, she pretends she's not. She pretends she's thirty. Hell, I don't mind. Never trust a woman who tells you her age. If she tells you that, she'll tell you anything. Wilde. Alice told me that one. She loved the theatre, Alice. Used to haul me along whenever she could. Personally, I preferred the opera. At least I could relax there, not have to think, you know. Even have the occasional forty winks. People could, if they saw you, imagine you were simply transported by the music and just had your eyes shut. How did I get on to that?"

"Patricia's age. You were talking about . . ."

"Look, Patricia's a real woman. I mean, she looks womanly. Alice didn't look womanly. Even after four children. She was too petite. Not voluptuous, like Patricia. No, Alice was a tiny little thing, like the shoes, which made her look younger. At least from the back. When she turned around, her face was more lined than one would have expected. More sad. I keep asking myself now, was she sad?"

"And what do you think?"

He looks out of the window, then looks back at me and shrugs his shoulders.

"I think . . . I think she was sad. I think she was sad . . . with me."

"And you? Were you happy with Alice?"

"I don't know. I just don't know. We had four children. There was a ten-year gap between Andrew, our eldest, and Barnaby, the baby. Baby Barnaby we used to call him, to tease him. And you know, that takes up thirty years of your life. If you're going to do it properly. And we wanted, Alice and I, we wanted very much to do it properly. And it was satisfying. It really was. But sometimes I think I was always looking at her over their heads. Just glimpsing her above this row, this gradation, of heads. Like a human bar chart. And mostly when we talked to each other, it was under a cascade of noise. Endless noise. Our marriage felt sort of drenched by them. And then it was over. The whole thing was over. They were gone. And then Alice died. And now, looking back on it, I think she was sad. And I'm frightened a bit, I think. Yes, I'm frightened. Is that the reason I'm here, do you think?

"I suppose you must talk to lots of people who are finding it hard to cope with memory and what's ahead. That's it, I suppose. How do I balance the two? I can't quite get the balance of the thing. So when Paul, you know, my GP, suggested I come to see you, I was insulted at first. But I hadn't been sleeping, not for months. And then the rages. The sudden rages. I'd exploded once or twice at work. Felt ashamed. So I rang him and said OK, I'll do it. Anyway, I'm glad now. I've found it helpful. I even managed to keep control over the weekend. More or less."

"What happened exactly? Were your friends difficult?"

"No, they weren't difficult. Apart from Tom's mother, who's hell to everyone. Tom was particularly welcoming, and his wife, Charlotte, was very kind. I've always liked her. She's sensible. She's a doctor, which impressed the hell out of me when I first met her. Handles Tom's nightmare of a mother very cleverly. Tom's mother's called Mary – inappropriately in my opinion - though, as Charlotte once said to me, Mary suits her. She thinks she's the Mother of God. Anyway, Mary wanted him to marry someone more glamorous, not so much – and this is what Charlotte believes – to be the daughter she never had, but to be a kind of co-conspirator in running her son's life. I told you she was clever, Charlotte.

"Adrian's wife is a different kettle of fish. She's glamorous, all right. She's his second wife. I remember having lunch with him at the Savoy, twelve or fourteen years ago I suppose, when he told me he was leaving Linda. He said he was mad for Helen. Mad for her. George, he said, you've no idea. I just have to look at her and I feel I'll die if I don't have her. I must have her. Look, George, he said, I hate men who talk about – you know – their women. It's one of the reasons we've always been such good friends. We haven't embarrassed each other or humiliated our wives. But George, he said, Helen's, well, I won't say more . . . but I went round to her flat the other day and she was wearing this black corset thing and nothing else.

"I wish he hadn't told me that. I couldn't get the image out of my mind. Came back every time I saw her. Anyway, on and on he went. George, he'd say, she's not one of those 'Why don't you stroke my hair, or some-thing,' you know, the tell-him-what-you-want school of sexual foreplay. George, you and I both know that when it's good, it's good, you don't need instruction. I just must be in the same room with Helen for the rest of my life. And even poor little Lucy and what I'm doing to her, leaving my six-year-old daughter, I'm lost, George.

"Well, he married Helen. He got her all right. I can't stand her. Well, I can just about take her once a year. They live in Chicago now. He's chairman of PTP Inc. Someone described him as the Don Juan of the board-room – endless take-overs. Still, I suppose the same rules apply. He earns a bloody fortune. He's got share options worth forty million dollars. Forty million! And an annual salary of two million! Can you believe it?"

"It's a lot of money."

"Hmm. Well, the row started when we were at dinner and Helen said she was going to Italy for a few days after the Grand Prix. This news surprised Adrian and things got a bit tense. Anyway, she left the table – lame excuse about a headache. And Mary said to Adrian, in this mocking way she has, Italy for a few days! You should have her followed, Adrian. Tom exploded at his mother. How in God's name can you say that to Adrian? Can't you see he's upset? And Adrian said very quietly, I don't need to have her followed, Mary. Helen leaves enough clues all over the house.

"Now you would think Mary'd lay off after that. It was plain the man was in agony. But oh no! Well, my dear Adrian, she said, you knew what you were getting into at the time. You married a ruthless young woman, who did not hesitate for an instant to seduce you away from your wife and small daughter. At which point Patricia, who should have kept her mouth firmly shut, considering she didn't really know anyone there, piped up, I suppose Adrian wasn't in any way responsible for leaving them. It was all Helen's fault, no doubt.

"There was a mortified silence and then Mary said, that's exactly what I'm saying, my dear. Women rule in this arena and all these painfully boring women's libbers – Mary's not exactly PC – who drone on and on about how badly men behave, should ask themselves, who do men leave women for? Baboons? No, my dear, they leave for another woman, who will pressure the man to come to the meanest deal he can with his previous family, so that there is the maximum available for the family she intends to have. I believe it's called the sisterhood. And 'twas ever thus, my dear young woman. What's your name again? I know it's not Alice . . . At which point Patricia got up and left the table."

"And you? What did you do?"

"I didn't follow her."

"Why not?"

"I didn't want to. I was angry with her."

"And?"

"And I realized in a way I really hadn't before, that she was never going to be like Alice. Ever. And, well, telling you now I suppose I understand that's what made me so angry."

"Because Patricia is not like Alice? Or because you are frightened that you cannot rely . . ."

"That's it! That's it exactly. Alice and I had worked out a kind of *modus operandi,* I suppose. I was at a dinner party the other night, and Francis Babbington, you know, ex-Arts Council guy, he's in industry now, was there with his new wife. She got carried away by something or other, Clause 28 I think. Started arguing with everyone. And poor Francis just didn't know whether to defend his wife, placate his client, or dazzle his potential sponsor for the House of Lords. His new wife, well, she's just so god-damn *sincere* about everything. Which is fine when you're at home, but my God, at a dinner party! I could *absolutely* rely on Alice not to make me look like a fool – you know? I suppose you could say we'd kind of trained each other . . ."

"And?"

"And . . . well, I suppose it's hard for me to accept that I'm just going to have to start again. That this is who I am now. All because I want Patricia. I want Patricia for the pleasure of sleeping with her. That's the truth, isn't it? And that's what's trapping me, even though I want it. But I suppose I must accept I'm the kind of man I never thought I'd be. I'm a man in his late fifties who wants to get into bed at night with a woman, a much younger woman, who is healthy. A woman who won't bloody die on me. Oh God, I'm crying again."

We sit in silence.

"I'd better leave now . . ."

We've time to spare – I'm not a believer in the fifty-minute hour. But he's anxious to get on with things.

". . . I'm seeing my middle son, Thomas, about a business matter. Shall I try to win him over to the idea of meeting Patricia? I think he's the most amenable . . ."

"What do you want to do?"

"I don't want to lose Patricia and I don't want to lose my children either. They're the last thirty years of my life. And I suppose they're all of Alice's. They're Alice's entire life, you see."

I walk him to the front door and, as we shake hands, he repeats:

". . . Alice's entire life," as though in disbelief.

As I open the door, two small children tumble out of a black Range Rover, followed by Ian Anderson, my first wife's second husband. They race past Sir George Bywater, who looks at them quizzically, and walks slowly down the steps and sinks into his chauffeur-driven Mercedes. As it speeds down Harley Street, he is no doubt lost in contemplation of Patricia, having lost Alice, the mother of his children. And I gaze down at Ellie's children, the trophies she won from Ian, when I shrank from being a father.

"Who was that?"

Margaret, skinny and pony-tailed, like her mother used to be, looks straight up at me, eyebrows arched in a way that's going to be fascinating when she's older.

"A patient."

"He didn't look sick."

"He's not."

"Then why's he here?"

"Good question. Come on up, you two. Ian, what time's your flight?"

"Nine. I can't stay to get them settled."

"We're not babies, Daddy." Margaret tosses her pony-tail.

"Mummy said you were no good with children. Which is why you didn't have any when you were married to her." Harry sounds alarmingly like Ian – even at six.

"Did she?"

"Oh God, Harry!" Ian sounds a little embarrassed – but only a little.

Laughter is best I think. Gratefully, Ian responds, the children follow his lead and we all laugh. Why not?

The children want to share a bedroom. Ian and I manoeuvre a sofa bed for Harry into the small guest-room next to mine and they promise they'll "settle down" later.

"Like babies?" he teases them.

"Oh, Daddy! And don't forget to give Mummy lots of hugs and kisses and tell her to hurry up and come home."

He gives them hugs and kisses of his own, then leaves to fly to his wife Ellie, who once was mine. The children look up at me, their mother's first husband; they are bemused. What are they to do with me? I am only of interest to them as a source of information about their mother. Like, will she get better quickly? She won't die, will she? Questions which they put in different guises all through supper.

They have their baths. I stand outside, as ordered. Finally, I get them into bed and read, very badly, a story about a dragon and two brave children who defy him, which Ian had thoughtfully packed for them. It's excruciatingly boring and since they know it by heart, I can't skip a word, never mind a line. I mention lights out, which strikes them as laughably quaint.

"We put our own lights out on our own special word of honour."

"Which is what?"

"It's a secret." Margaret beams at me.

"Well, how will I know without coming to check?"

"You'll have to trust us."

"Does Mummy always trust you to put your lights out?"

"Always."

A pause, and then from Margaret, "You didn't love Mummy enough to stay with her, isn't that right?"

I hesitate.

She continues, warming to her theme, which is an old one, "That's what she told us. That it wasn't just about children. Well, actually, she told Harry and Harry told me. Harry tells me everything."

And I think, watch out, Harry, that's a very bad habit you've got there.

"Mummy never lies to us." Harry again. Oh Harry, are you going to have trouble when you grow up!

"Well, if Mummy told you that, it must be right."

"Daddy and Mummy love each other a lot. But I suppose that was well after you."

"Yes . . . well after me," I lie.

"It was a whole year."

"Mummy told you that?"

"Yes, she did."

"And Mummy never lies." Harry, again. "You're all alone now, Mummy says. Poor old you. We can't stay, you know. We have to go when Granny comes for us in the morning."

"He doesn't care, dummy. He doesn't like children." Margaret, the forthright.

21

"Oh, I think I could make an exception for you two."

"No, don't! We really can't stay here with you. We're going home to our own house when Daddy comes back with Mummy. Then we'll all be together again. That's true, isn't it?" Margaret, the vulnerable.

"Yes, that's true. Good-night, Margaret. Good-night, Harry. I'm in the next room. I'll leave the door open."

"We're not babies."

"Of course not."

"But leave the lights on in the corridor . . . that's all."

Two

—

SATURDAY, SIX a.m. Rose, Ellie's mother, ringing from her car, wakes me with the minimum of courtesy and absolutely no apology. This has often been described as "Rose's style". Since it has remained remarkably consistent over the years, few are offended and, indeed, many welcome it. "At least she's honest, darling. You know where you stand with Rose." But then people's desire to be wounded is almost insatiable and Rose provides an up-front service.

"You've got the children?"

"You make it sound as though I kidnapped them."

"Well, maybe secretly you'd like to. After all, they could have been yours."

"Never analyse an analyst, Rose."

"But you're crying out for it, darling. It's clear to anyone. The reason I'm so blithe this morning, after a totally hellish journey undertaken without Richard who had to stay on to finish the conference, is I've just spoken to Ian and it's all much less serious than they feared. He's panicked us all. And not for the first time. God, I preferred your neurosis. Much more interesting. And you are after all, my sweet, my very first son-in-law. One always remains rather attached to the first . . . don't you think?"

"Thanks, Rose. And I've caught the under-note."

"Clever boy! I'm sure Ian persuaded her to go to the hospital, when all she was probably suffering from was

23

tension. Perhaps being away from the children brought it on. But my God, it's only for a fortnight. People make such a big deal of it nowadays. When I was . . . ah well, I'll continue to fascinate you over breakfast. I'm ravenous. And, of course, you can tell me all your problems. It can be a case of 'come to mother-in-law'. Bye."

"Goodbye, Rose."

Rose was a shock when I first met her. Always look at the mother, they say, that's your girlfriend in twenty years' time. She had, she'd confided to me once, travelled around Europe "on the oldest passport in the world. Beauty, darling, beauty. Long legs helped, of course." I refused to look shocked and thereby passed a kind of test. She liked to disconcert people, casually throwing out remarks such as, "Thank God Hitler was anti-Semitic, otherwise Germany would have won the war." As the stunned listener tried to prepare a suitable response, she would continue, "He lost all the best scientists, darling, who were Jewish, naturally. Between 1909 and 1932 Germany won thirty-three out of one hundred Nobel prizes for science. During the next twenty-three years, sweetie, it won eight – three of them shared."

She was the daughter of an English civil servant, who during a posting to Berlin had become "enchanted", as she put it, by her German Jewish mother. He managed in 1939 to get his wife, Astrid, and their six-year-old daughter back to London. Ten years later, with petulant ingratitude, the gloriously beautiful Astrid left what to her was now a rather boring husband, for an Italian count she met at an embassy party, who believed in *la dolce vita*. The hapless Rose trailed along in her wake. Her father died a few months later – "Broken heart? I don't think so, darling." His legacy to Rose was what she described as "proper English". "I learned the three 'ics' – as my father called them – early. The essential key to the true English language style – which is 'ironic, laconic, satiric'. I know I never get it *quite* right, but I do try, darling, I do try." Rose had added a dash of black humour – "from my mother, sweetie" – before the whole bilingual exercise got caught up in a slightly more depressing game of inter-personal relations – betrayal, divorce and death. Rose's mother and the count died when she was seventeen, in what she described as "a quite ridiculous boating accident".

So there was Rose, now a teenager, orphaned and "though I say so myself, absolutely gorgeous". She was snapped up pretty quickly, nineteen to be exact, she told me, by an old friend of the count. And thus began her career as a wife to a series of trophy husbands. She lived in one of Rome's loveliest *palazzi*, for four years, no children, "his fault, I think, darling"; a château in the Dordogne, "my favourite, alas for only seven years". The French aristocrat, unlike his Italian predecessor, made Rose a mother which she "simply adored". However, for all her worldly cunning, she'd been, as she put it, "out-manoeuvred by a very clever Scandinavian". She considered this defeat to be "absolutely amazing. I'd never found them to be all that bright. Anyway, I always knew he'd leave me for someone else and he was perfectly generous." She and Ellie moved to Madrid with the art collector Edward Bewley, to a villa which she found to be not very grand, but "authentic, definitely authentic". She only truly slummed it once, she told me, "for love, of course. Well, sex actually. Pure sex" with a German, in Munich. Though it was a vast apartment it was not *quite* what she was used to. The pure sex with the German lawyer, which had ended the third marriage, did not result in his request for her hand.

She felt she'd done Europe, and she knew her sentimental education was over. So she packed her languages and all that she'd learned about the finest furniture, paintings and *objets d'art* in Europe into a kind of mental holdall, and with her only real treasure, Ellie, she took on London. "And I honestly think, darling, I won. As for the husbands and lovers, somehow, I'm still not sure how, exactly, God, it's so complicated, I just lost all of them along the way. Richard, of course, is absolutely unlosable. Very reassuring at my age."

It was as a result of the various marriages and liaisons that Ellie – no doubt having inherited Rose's gift – was fluent in four languages and in addition spoke the "adequate Spanish". So Rose had brought her linguistically over-educated daughter to England and set up her now hugely successful interior design business. She specialized, she told me, in bringing out the soul of rich people's houses. And it was the word "soul" that particularly appealed to me. Some years after her arrival, she'd settled into the liaison with Richard. "God, I'm so embarrassed, another lawyer, but English, darling. They're definitely more reliable."

Hers was a tale with a rather curious glamour, brilliantly told, and it elicited precisely the response which Rose desired – amused confusion. She fascinated but she did not convince. To delve deeper would clearly be exhausting, and since human beings' interest in each other is more limited than we care to believe, Rose's story achieved the icy purity and cathedral-like structure of an ornate wedding-cake. One which no one really wished to dismantle. Least of all me. Some of Rose's history was probably not true. But then, better the lie you can live with.

She had entered my life when I was twenty-five and determined, absolutely determined, to marry her daughter. Since my divorce from Ellie, which, notwithstanding the fact she was pregnant by another man, Rose believed to be entirely my fault, my extraordinary mother-in-law had bullied me into seeing her every few months for dinner *à deux*. I could, of course, have refused, but I surrendered. I was well aware of the ambiguities inherent in my acquiescence.

Now she comes for Ellie's children, who are asleep upstairs in the room adjacent to mine. A room, though I did not tell them, their mother had once used as her study.

Three

——

"GOD, THIS is a dreary house!"

Rose has arrived. Her height, five-eleven in high heels which she always wears, her daunting chic – "always couture, best possible investment the older woman can make" – heavy, dark blonde hair and cleverly made-up face, mean that even now, in her late sixties, she can and does make an entrance. And that's before she launches into "Rose-speak".

"So you've told me before, Rose. You don't look a bit tired."

"Maddening, isn't it?" This is Rose's way of accepting a compliment.

"My grandchildren still asleep?"

"Yes. At least, I haven't heard a sound from them."

"That doesn't mean they're sleeping. No idea, have you, Jack?"

"None."

"I'll go up and check them, shall I?"

"No, I'll go."

I need a breathing space before Rose launches into the verbal stripping of the walls, design assassination of the curtains, carpets and furniture of the entire house, which is her mission on the rare occasions she has been in the house since the divorce. Though in a perverse way, I quite enjoy these attacks.

The children are fast asleep. I creep downstairs again and as I walk in . . .

"You haven't changed the kitchen much."

I smile. The game has begun. We are practised players at this style of social intercourse which has served us so well in the past. The persona in which Rose is most comfortable with me, is that of audacious critic of my interior decorating style. I am aware that I must play the role of hopeless male, the sterility of whose current single status is accurately reflected in the banal design of his kitchen. A room whose horror is matched only by what she once described as the unspeakable putty-colour of my sitting-room.

"For God's sake, Jack. I mean, honestly, you've done nothing, absolutely nothing, with this room for what – ten years? Maybe more."

"That's because I got it right at the beginning."

I'm not certain if Rose is aware that I have only ever lived in two houses. This one and the one I was born into. I am faithful to houses, and this house is it for me. Like a good marriage, this domiciliary love requires exclusive attention. Rose might be surprised to find out that in fact I am very responsive to the moods of my house. I understand its resentments; I am aware that it loathes fancy dress or changes of style. But then, Rose would never understand that. She is relentless in her passion for redecoration.

"I could have advised you. It *is* my business, after all, Jack. If you wouldn't listen to Ellie, you could at least have listened to me."

"Ellie was perfectly happy with the house, Rose. Scrambled eggs OK?"

In fact, as I now understand, Ellie was not at all happy

with the house. However, during the five years she lived here, regularly broken by tours to various provincial theatres, she loyally resisted all efforts by Rose to redecorate. I was grateful, of course, but I also expected this acquiescence. It was my house. I was conscious of the unfairness of my attitude. But being aware of something and having any intention of acting on one's awareness, are two entirely different things. A fact of life of which I am daily apprised.

My contribution, in order as I saw it to balance the scales, was to accept that Ellie had not the slightest interest in organising domestic matters and that cooking was, to her, a total bore. We ate more salads than even the most committed health guru would regard as strictly necessary. In the winter, her main concession to the drop in temperature was to precede the salad with a good warming soup, tins of which she kept neatly stacked in alphabetical order in the cupboard in the kitchen. Unlike David Copperfield and his hopeless Dora, I found this aspect of Ellie endearing. Besides, if your mother is famous for the stylish way she runs her house and the quality of her table, then what self-respecting daughter would not down her wooden spoons?

"Mmmm. I don't think she was. After all, you changed virtually nothing after Kate left and Ellie moved in. But perhaps that was change enough?"

"Stop the amateur psychology, Rose. Have some coffee?"

"Yes, please."

Rose lingers on "please" in a way that reminds me of Ellie.

"I think I'm going to need it. Looking at your expression, darling, not to mention the ghastly walls in this charmless room, I'll probably need at least two or three more cups before we're through. Sorry to be so frank, darling, but you know me."

"Do I, Rose?" as I put the scrambled eggs before her.

She looks at them, astonished that I am capable of preparing this most basic of dishes, and even manages a thank-you before continuing:

"What on earth can you mean? We've known each other for years. You were my first, my adored, son-in-law. God, how I wish I had you back again safely in the bosom of my family. I'm like the child of divorced parents, darling. I harbour dreams that you two will make up and get back together again. Though, of course, rather unusually, I do not suffer any feelings of guilt for having been so bad that 'daddy left mummy'."

She smiles her Rose smile and raises the magnificent Rose eyebrows, and continues, "I am right, aren't I, Jack? Some children do feel badly. They believe they're responsible for the break-up, even when, of course, they have nothing to feel guilty about at all. Or have I got all this wrong? Women's-magazine standard, I'm afraid."

"Don't underestimate yourself, Rose. You're formid-able in many, many ways."

"Thank you, Jack. I think that might be the first com-pliment you've ever paid me. I shall treasure it. Now that Ellie's going to be all right, and I can plead jet lag for what I'm going to say – why do you think Ellie finally left you?"

"I know why she left me."

"Do you, dear? I don't think so."

"It may pain you, Rose, but Ellie left me because of Ian and certain tensions between us concerning children."

I resist the desire to say because she was pregnant, and not by me.

"Absolute rubbish! And you know it. Just this once during our unexpected early morning get-together – see it as a dawn raid, darling – I'm going to get straight to the point."

"And you're normally so reticent . . ."

She glances at me sharply but sarcasm is not going to deflect her. How could I have imagined it would.

"Ellie left because of Kate, of course! It was intolerable. Absolutely intolerable. I mean, the phone calls – sometimes in the middle of the night. Her turning to you about every goddamn decision she ever made. Her psychological presence never left this house. Which is why you should have damn well redecorated when I told you to."

"Redecoration is not the answer to everything, Rose."

"Don't you be too sure. You can be quite patronising sometimes, Jack. That sister of yours has been spinning a web around you all her life and she caught my Ellie in it. Oh, I know what you're going to say. God knows we've hedged round this often enough. Ellie had an affair and deliberately became pregnant. But that was all *your* fault for not dealing finally with Kate. As for redecorating, I spent my youth redecorating myself, changing styles, presenting myself to the world in a way which would make it possible for me to survive. For which I make no apologies. I could make a damn good ethical case for hedonism. It helped me on the journey from horror to a perfectly acceptable, perfectly frivolous life. For which, may I say, I am very grateful. I do no harm and therefore forgive myself for the fact that I don't do very much good either. In fact, looking at the history of the countries in which I spent my youth, I think a harmless, frivolous life is a bloody triumph. There! Know me better now?"

This is a different Rose. I haven't heard her in a self-justifying mode before. I turn my chair at an angle towards her, an old habit, and say, "Well . . ."

But her question was rhetorical.

"I know, darling," she continues. "I'm that boring cliché, a survivor. We're a species boring to everyone who hasn't put in the hours talking themselves back to life. My dearest friend at the time, much cleverer than me, used to say it was like ripping off layers of memory, the way a drowning man struggles out of his clothes in order to get to the surface. Because the seabed is not a natural place to be. Think of all the minor mistakes you can make on a boat, without catastrophe. But when you're in a submarine, Jack, you better get every little thing right or you'll never get to the surface again. But I don't have to tell you that, do I? You know the score, Jack. You know the lower depths do nothing for the soul except teach it that it doesn't ever, ever want to go back there."

"Oh, come on, Rose. Three marriages is hardly the lower depths."

"Ah, the marriages! I learned that the men who married me did not fall victim to my charms in order to enjoy a crash course in my traumatic history. And besides, everyone wanted to forget history then. My husbands and lovers showed a certain lack of interest, shall we say, in my mind.

"And over the years, I colluded in all this denial. Perhaps I didn't really want to share those secret things with anyone. Even now, I don't want to wear my history like some unusual choker around my neck so that people can say, 'Rose, dear, where on earth did you get that? It's so . . . so unusual. You're so clever at finding these things.'"

Is it the jet lag or does Rose actually sound sincere? Before I can decide she's off again.

"I must stop. I'm here for breakfast and to pick up my grandchildren, not for a special family-rate consultation. I've probably said too much already. But early morning, after a shock – and let's be fair, Jack, we've both had a bit of a fright about Ellie – can be a time for confidences. I think I actually feel a bit embarrassed now. Can that be possible, darling?"

"It'll pass, Rose. It will pass."

Much of her energy is an act of will. No doubt exhausting on a day-in, day-out basis. She's the kind of woman you'd be delighted to find yourself sitting beside at dinner. But well before coffee, you'd be glad to get away. All that daunting repartee – and she probably sings in the morning!

"You know, Jack, I regard my life as a minor masterpiece. Even the divorces were not too ghastly for Ellie. Just look at her. She's not only brilliant in her field; she's a sensible, tough girl who lives a sensible life with her husband and children. The wildest thing she ever did in her life was to leave you. A mistake, I think. She could have worked on you a bit more."

"Worked on me?"

"Yes, worked on you. I would have helped her if she'd let me. But I took you at face value when I first met you. I allowed myself to be blinded by my daughter's happiness. Indeed, I *wanted* to be blinded by it. Because it proved to me that I'd done well. You and Ellie, well, it was all so normal. I adore normal! Normal to me is a miracle. And Kate seemed to me then to be just a strangely beautiful girl who adored her brother. It even added to your charms in the beginning. Everything happened so fast. I barely got a chance to talk to Edmund, about what you were like as children, what your mother was like, why he adopted you both. But no, with all my experience, I simply let love find its way. And then, of course, you blew it – to use an expression of which her second husband is inordinately fond."

"And you blame Kate?"

"Well, I blame *you* for not handling Kate properly. I don't care what little secret you two are covering up. It's nothing I won't have seen before, I can assure you."

"This early morning chat may be getting a little out of hand, Rose."

"Sorry, I ought to come clean. It's not just because of you and Ellie, and my love, unrequited – no, don't deny it – for my ex-son-in-law. Now, I've heard Kate's got Harold Abst in her clutches. His uncle is an old friend of mine. So was his father. Harold is hugely clever, of course, but he's cursed with a sensual nature. Kate's his type, all right. That wretched air of mystery which men find so compelling has made him awfully susceptible. I think Harold should get to know her better."

Rose's vocal emphasis on "that wretched air of mystery" underlines her resentment of a seasoned player in an arena she once dominated, one whose strategy remains irritatingly opaque. Perhaps unconsciously she feels that Kate's beauty played some part in what she saw as a defeat of her own daughter, Ellie. A daughter whose determinedly low-key presentation of her female power constantly mystified Rose, even though it had the benefit that she never experienced inter-generational competition. Which can be quite a bitter coming-of-age for the celebrated older beauty.

"I'm not going to get angry with you, Rose – but what you're suggesting sounds vaguely insulting. Not to mention the madness of interfering in the marital plans of a middle-aged man."

"Really? How long have you been a psychiatrist? It's the marital plans of the middle-aged man which most need investigation. A man in his fifties – late fifties to be exact – contemplating marriage to a much younger woman is the ultimate proof of the inequality of the sexes. Young female predator, with ageing lion in her sights, may indeed be seeking wealth and position in marriage. But the man, poor, poor darling, is seeking nothing less than the reinvention of himself. What is more seductive? He becomes younger, of course. A veritable baby with all those new things to learn from this new woman. First of all the physical remodelling, the hair-style which is so much more flattering to him. The diet with the ultimate incentive – sexual reward. There isn't a woman in the world that doesn't know how to play this little game. Suddenly the poor man finds himself in a new life of increasing energy, minimum restraint. Laughter, for God's sake.

"I will admit that Kate isn't typical, though. Which makes her more lethal. For the record, she's totally knocked daughters of friends out of the running. Mothers in London are in mourning. Harold's quite a catch, you know. Mind you, there's a glut of young women in the market at the moment, which would make the problems of that mother with all the daughters . . . marvellous movie with Greer Garson . . . what was the mother called?"

"Mrs. Bennet . . ."

"That's it! Mrs. Bennet's problems would fade into insignificance now. London is awash; it's drowning, in these marvellous, elegant creatures, educated, clever – at least at their jobs, darling. They all want to be loved for their minds, not all of them first-class. But where, oh where, are the men that can match them? None of these girls can beat Kate. I know a player when I see one. What Kate exudes is secrecy, mystery. Absolutely irresistible to a man like Harold, who believes he knows everything. And another——"

The phone rings.

"That's probably Ian," I say, thankful for the interruption.

I pick up the phone. Ian's voice has its usual high-irritant quotient. I try to sound friendly.

"Jack. Everything all right?"

"No problems, Ian. Rose is here. How's Ellie?"

"Much better. They think it was stress and they've found she's a bit anaemic. We're so relieved. She's sleeping now. We'll be coming home day after tomorrow. Simon, the assistant director, has stepped in. Everybody's being incredibly nice about it. There's someone else in the company with pretty fluent French and Italian. So everything is OK. Otherwise Ellie'd feel so guilty. I feel terrible myself about panicking Rose the other night, but I was just incredibly worried."

"Want to speak to her?"

"Yes, please."

"All's well," I mouth to her as she takes the phone.

She is kinder than I expect and, after an agreement that she will take the children after breakfast and a promise to ring in a couple of hours, she puts the phone down.

"He's just . . . just so . . . what's the word I'm looking for, darling?"

"Oh no, Rose! I'm not going down that path."

"Meanie! OK, let's get those treasures out of bed and feed them. Where did you put them? In the attic?"

"In the small room beside mine."

"Oh good, I'm longing to see your bedroom again," she says, with a kind of mocking emphasis on the word "longing".

"I thought you might be."

Suddenly, the doorbell rings.

"Who could that be? It's a bit early for a patient."

"It's Saturday, Rose."

"Of course it is. It must be the jet lag. My body can take it, but not my mind."

And Kate's voice comes over the entry phone . . .

"It's me . . ."

I want to greet her away from Rose's ferocious gaze.

"Back in a minute."

I race down the stairs and there she is in the hallway, looking concerned and slightly nervous. She speaks quickly.

"I'm sorry. I wasn't at the flat last night. I came back early this morning, you know how I like to, and got your message. I tried to ring, you were engaged, so I came straight round. How's Ellie?"

"She's fine. It was stress-exhaustion. She collapsed, and you know Ian . . ."

"No, not really. I'm glad she's OK. Where are the children?"

"Upstairs. Rose is here."

"Oh God . . ."

"Don't worry. She's leaving soon. Taking them to 'Granny's'."

"Hard to imagine her in that role."

Kate precedes me up the stairs into the kitchen. Rose, leaning back in her chair, raises her eyebrows in the way Margaret, demonstrating genetic inheritance at its most subtle, did last night.

"Ah, Kate. How lovely you look. Even in the cold, early morning. But then pale pink cashmere is so flattering to the skin and your marvellous red hair tumbling down in that wildly attractive way . . . You are, as they say nowadays, what is it they say . . . a knockout?"

"I'm so relieved Ellie's all right. You must have been very worried."

"Oh, I've been *much* more worried in the past about Ellie. I had a feeling Ian was exaggerating. He doesn't like her being away, you see."

"I'm glad they're so happy."

"I'm sure you are. Well, I'd better get the children. I heard the other day that you may be getting married again, to Harold Abst. Or is that just gossip?"

I look at Kate. She's been so good so far, not responding to Rose's mean little provocations.

"I don't know, Rose. It's possible. But we haven't made a decision yet."

"We? *We* haven't made a decision yet? And to which 'we' are you referring?"

"Rose!" I stop her there. "I'm terribly fond of you but I think I'm going to take you upstairs right now. We'll get the children and you can peep in and crucify the new colour scheme in my bedroom. You can have a field day."

"Thank you, darling. That would cheer me up. Now,

you carry that jug of orange juice; I'll take the glasses. They can have their juice upstairs and then Granny will take them out for a big-treat breakfast at Selfridge's. After that, we'll hit Hamley's for a few hours, then home to Carlyle Square. Lizzie can do them lunch and I'll put them in front of a video and Granny can have a rest."

"Can I help?"

Rose takes charge. "No, dear. You just sit and have your coffee. We'll be down soon."

Margaret and Harry are no longer asleep, but lying in their beds, whispering to each other. They stop as we walk in and look at us a little dazed. Adults are now in the room and Margaret and Harry in the blinking of their eyes have closed off their real world.

They sit straight up and launch into a torrent of questions about Mummy.

"Is she better?"

"When is she coming back?"

"Will we all be together soon?"

"Mummy's going to be fine. She and Daddy are coming back on Monday." Rose, in reassuring grandmother mode. She's good at it.

"Is that a promise?"

"That's a promise. Now what about a kiss for Grandma?"

"Have you told Jack you're going to take us away? We know he's lonely, but we have to go."

"Oh yes, Jack knows. But Jack's sister is here. So he'll be OK."

"We didn't know you had a sister."

"Yes, we did, Harry. Mummy says she was famous once. She was the Running Girl . . ."

I decide not to correct her. After all, what's the

difference? Walking, running? Kate's always been leaving . . .

"Now, Mummy says, she writes fluffy things in fluffy magazines."

"What's a fluffy thing?" asks Harry.

"Look." Margaret leaps out of bed, swings her dressing-gown around her like a cloak and minces her way to the mirror. She then mimics an extravagantly careful application of lipstick, turns around and says:

"Do you think this colour is . . . ME?"

Beaming at us, she continues. "I saw that in a movie the other night, which our nanny, who's just had her 'pendicitis out, let us watch. Anyway, *that's* a fluffy thing, Harry."

"Oh," says Harry.

"Our mummy's in the theatre. She does radio now, 'cos of us. But she says Art is what matters, and our daddy looks after poor people. *Our* mummy and daddy don't do fluffy things."

Even though they're only children, something in their tone grates on my moral ear. Or is it simply that I resent, even from children, any implied criticism of Kate and the elective superficialities of her life? Ian rather over-eggs the piety bit in describing his job as a senior director of Social Services for a trendy North London borough, as a St-Francis-of-Assisi role, distributing alms to the needy. A set of parents, now grandparents, had of course made generous contributions to the holy family of NW1. This meant that life on the front line of virtue was not lacking in certain little essentials – decent house, car, private education fund in place for the little angels. Nevertheless, the message was clear to their children: if you can't be an Artist, be Worthy.

Far from finding Ellie's tough, sexy puritanism unattractive, I had always found this aspect of her appealing. The fact that her high moral tone had not in any way prevented her from becoming pregnant with Ian's child while still married to me became, over time, a cause less of censure and more of sadness. And I bear my own responsibility. I missed every signal that she gave me. The way that doctors are famously blind to symptoms within their own families.

Rose smiles mockingly, as I take Harry to the bathroom and wait outside, as ordered. Rose and Margaret follow and, after tears from Margaret because Daddy had not packed her "Saturday red tights", but her "rubbishy grey school ones", and Harry's left shoe is eventually found, they drink their orange juice. Then they carefully start a list of what they'd like from Hamley's. And I suddenly think of George and Alice and all those years spent on that escalator from nought to eighteen, or whatever age it is they leave home. Running up, and then down a few steps, as a new child joined on the first step. Trying to get each one safely to the top. And, having deposited the last child at the top, did they look down at the now empty escalator and wonder why no trace at all was left?

"Jack, you've not done so badly in this room . . ." Rose's voice from my bedroom:

". . . Monastic grey walls, cream curtains. Well done. And the Biedermeier sofa . . . it's quite . . . quite stylish. Yes, I can truthfully say it's quite stylish. Though I notice it's still the same old bed. No change there."

I smile. What else is there to do?

"Thank you, Rose. Shall we go?"

And we trail down to the kitchen. Our arms are laden with Gap holdalls, navy for Harry, red for Margaret; a sinister-looking, furry animal and a doll, sporting a miniature version of the weird little boots Ellie used to wear.

"Hello." Kate stands up when they come into the room, as though she's standing to attention.

"You're Jack's sister? You don't look like him."

"Well, you don't look like me either, Harry. Brothers and sisters never look alike."

"Oh yes they do. Billy and Jennie at school do."

"They're twins, dummy."

"Children, we must be off. Jack, you've handled this invasion remarkably well. I'll tell Ellie. She'll be fascinated. And Kate, Harold Abst might suit you very well indeed. I know his uncle. And his father, sadly dead now, was a very shrewd man. Worldly, not fazed by anything. I've heard Harold is quite like him."

Rose does the eyebrow-arching thing again; the action seems not just a distinguishing mark of physiognomy but a Dali-like symbol of something extreme in Rose, which goes far beyond her waspish speech.

Then they are gone. Rose had been collected from the airport and all three settle down in the back of a large red Jaguar – a perfect Rose car. She and the children disappear down an almost empty Saturday-morning Harley Street, both its healers and its wounded having a rest.

Kate is playing with a strand of her hair and looking out of the kitchen window when I get back.

"Rose is right, of course – she's right about me."

"How do you mean?"

"Well, the automatic way that even in a rush I'd pick out the most flattering colour to wear when I'm tired."

"Are you tired?"

"Don't be so kind to me, Jack. I'm attempting a little

self-awareness here. I'm trying to tell you that Rose is right. I'm vain."

"That's not what she said."

"Well, it's what she meant. The other night Mark Carter, who's got Important Politician emblazoned on his forehead, spent the evening telling me what a glorious creature I am. The fact that Harold was sitting exactly opposite him did not prevent him whispering to me when he could, that my face entranced him. That I was so-o-o beautiful. Does he think I don't know?"

"Men probably think you like to be told."

"Oh, I do like to be told. Of course I do. And I look after this particular inheritance. I'll give you my routine, Jack. It's a lot more sophisticated than when you and I were young."

She stops suddenly. As we usually do when we talk of when we were young. We look at each other, and smile that smile we both know so well. Then we look away and she continues with the much safer subject of the vanity of beautiful women.

"You could say it was my job. Every morning I brush my entire body, standing naked in front of my mirror. I see a reflection that is like a painting. Honestly, I astonish myself. I start with the soles of my feet, then I move up along my legs and thighs, across my stomach, in circular movements over my hips. Then along my palms, across my shoulders and down my back. As much as possible I brush towards the heart. Perhaps it helps to keep it beating."

I say nothing.

"Jack, pay attention. This is a master class in something or other. I'll remember what later. Now, where was I? Oh yes, my bath, I was about to step into my bath, which is filled with oil of roses. I do not slide down, completely under the water. That is my daily triumph of the will. Then I get out, I dry myself and I put on three, yes three, different lotions. Moisturising, tightening for my hips and stomach, and a firming foam on my breasts. Then I deodorize myself. I get my pale-rose knickers and bra, it's my favourite colour scheme – and after that I roll up my stockings, I never wear tights, which shows, don't you think, that I am quite serious about all this, no? And I pull on my dress, or skirt and sweater, and *voilà*! My nakedness is covered. You think that's it?"

"I hope so, Kate."

She is speaking of her language of the flesh, the hygiene of the self.

"Oh, dear me, no. Twice a week I have my hair done. Once a week my nails, on my hands, not my feet. That's another schedule. Fortnightly. Plus my facial and my massage and waxing. Oh, I forgot my personal trainer Ron, twice a week at the Dorchester. I am a perfect vessel. And this is a perfectly legitimate version of me. It is the body that I live in. Live on in? Can you say that? It doesn't seem quite right . . ."

Sometimes, when I hear the under-note, I feel I should just take off with her and protect her all my life. Which I know is not her safest option.

As if she reads my thoughts, she suddenly switches the conversation:

"He wants to see you. To talk to you properly."

"Oh Kate, is it necessary? I mean, do I have to?"

"He wants to marry me. He wants a decision soon."

"Of course he does."

"Can I do it?"

"You asked me that the last time, Kate."

"You said yes the last time."

"It seemed right then."

"For me or for André?"

"Kate, I did the duty nearest to me. Which was to concentrate on what was best for you. It's the closest I get to a moral code."

"And I was playing for time," she says. It's a game she started young.

"Maybe . . . I saw André's mother the other night."

"Virginia? Virginia's in London?"

"Well, she was a few nights ago. She was at one of those charity dinners. Save the Rhino, something like that."

"What on earth were you doing there?"

"I was making a peace offering. I'd behaved badly. My punishment was to endeavour to save the poor rhino."

"Who is she, the one who required the peace offering?"

"No one important."

"And what's the name of the unimportant one?"

"Cora."

Cora is the young woman who believes that she is having a relationship with me. The word "relationship" adds a certain *gravitas* which I do not believe our liaison merits. That the nature of the affair has been made clear to her is irrelevant. Women's intuition is an overrated commodity, particularly when it clashes with their will.

I'd arrived late at the charity dinner. This rather defeated the purpose of my attending in the first place, which was to make an emollient gesture to Cora. I'd smiled at her when she glared at me from the other side of the large table and I'd turned my attention to the lady on my right. Her passion for the rhino was positively evangelical. I was swept up in a mass of statistical information, laced with physiological detail about the animal, which should be assigned to the domain of learned journals for veterinarian surgeons. I'd turned with relief to my left and Virginia Bronfman, realizing that I had not recognized her, curved her elegant fingers over my placement card and reminded me that we'd met before.

"And what did Virginia say?" Kate's voice seems anxious.

"Nothing much."

"Liar."

"To tell you the truth, I didn't recognize her immediately."

"Well, that's unlike you. Perhaps you were still feeling guilty about the unimportant one? So tell me, what did Virginia have to say?"

"Well, after she'd reminded me pointedly that you'd once been married to her son, she emphasized that she considered it an 'unwise' marriage."

"She's right, of course. But I hope you defended me."

"Yes, your knight in shining armour implied that perhaps André felt it wise at the time. Though I felt sorry the minute I'd said it. She looked very sad and she said that he didn't think it was wise at the time. That he thought it was essential. Which she regarded as an entirely different matter. She's an impressive woman really, and he is her only son."

"Did she mention how André is now?"

"Virginia approves of the new wife. They've got twin boys now. I gather their empire in Sydney is expanding. In fact they see Australia as the first step towards the Asian market. The Bronfman dynasty extracts quite a price from those trapped within it."

"I'm glad he's happy." She smiles radiantly at me.

"She didn't say he was happy. Did you know that after you left him he didn't speak at all for a month? His father begged him to see a doctor, evidently. They were distraught. They were afraid they would lose him, was how she put it to me. Then Virginia said something very interesting. She said "Giving birth is nothing. What is required of parents is dedication to the art of helping their children save their own lives." She made it clear she was not referring to telling them to fasten their seat-belts, or to be careful crossing the road. Then she asked me, did I ever tell my patients that?"

"What did you say?"

"I said no. She told me to remember it for the next relevant occasion."

I decide not to tell Kate what she'd said next. "You see, Jack, my son, whom your sister described in an interview once as a nice young man she'd married too young, was in love; incandescently, dangerously, in love with your sister. Whose name I sometimes cannot bring myself to utter. Tell me, Jack, have you ever been incandescently in love?" To which I had no answer. She'd been about to say something else when silence was requested. The young woman on my right, whose life is currently dedicated to the salvation of the rhino, picked her way, in what seemed like a cloud of lilac silk, to the microphone and started her lengthy oration. At the end of which, as the speaker floated from the podium to thunderous applause, Virginia Bronfman slipped away. The rest of the evening was, alas, passed by Cora and me in the social purgatory that rowing couples inflict on one another.

"That's about it, Kate. Then we moved on to the rhino."

She sees I'm tired and, ruffling my hair as she passes my chair, says, "I'll go now. Promise me you'll come tonight. Come early. Seven o'clock. That way you can talk to Harold before anyone arrives. You see, Jack, I feel that he could build a wall around me and that I could hide behind it."

I say nothing.

She sighs, then looking away from me and in that tone I know so well, she whispers, "I'm sinking again. I'm sinking. Please, Jack. Please."

She leans against me and I stroke her hair. Eventually she says in that tone of voice, which always moves me, "Ah well. Ah well."

I walk her to the front door. I'm suddenly exhausted. Ellie, Ian, their children, Rose, Virginia, too many people and too much of the past has crowded in on me in the space of twenty-four hours. The effect is fugue-like. I lean against the door-frame and gaze at her.

"Please, Jack," she whispers again.

I close my eyes and, of course, as always, I say:

"Yes."

Four

—

THE NIGHT before her first marriage, I drove to Geneva from Paris where I'd attended a series of lectures on Lacan. I was particularly interested in the theory of *stade du miroir*, that essential stage of self-discovery in reflection; in our century in mirrors, in previous centuries in water, or even wine. My French, in which I had previously taken great pride, even occasionally competing with Ellie, had not proved itself adequate to the full comprehension of the lectures. I was mentally exhausted, therefore, when I started the long drive to Geneva. I surrendered to the physical pleasures of speed and arrived, in a strange way, refreshed.

André's parents wished to hold the reception in the famous hotel in which their only son had spent his seemingly blossom-laden childhood, gazing at Geneva's lakes, mountains and tax-advantaged citizens. They believed in the sunny life. One of the few intimate things André's mother ever said to me, was that her husband required her to be happy, particularly during those endless sunny days, when he regarded clouds of human unhappiness with the same distaste as their meteorological cousins.

As the bride's procession from the parental home was not possible for Kate, she'd smiled her acquiescence to the choice of Geneva for the wedding. This no doubt had further convinced her young husband-to-be of the wisdom of his choice.

The news of their engagement appeared in the diary section of one of the tabloids, in advance of the formal announcement in *The Times*. She'd sent it to me with a scrawled, combined question and exclamation mark. The piece, accompanied by a photograph in which little could be discerned other than teeth and smiles, devoted a paragraph to the "shock and anguish" of the aristocratic young woman to whom André had previously been engaged.

Evidently Clarissa something-or-other had declared when her own engagement to André had been announced, that she intended making up for the centuries-old tradition of her class of not educating "gels" by putting her terrifying double-first from Oxford to use in the London branch of an American bank. She also, rather rashly, stated that at the same time she intended to produce "at least five children".

Whether Kate's father-in-law-to-be, who'd spent his life building his hotel and catering empire, was quite so thrilled by his son's decision to forgo the still not inconsiderable advantages of marrying into the aristocracy, was another matter. If he had misgivings he hid them well. Perhaps he'd seen enough of life to know that once a man has succumbed to the delirium of the soul and senses promised by the vision of a particular woman, there is no saving him.

When I'd arrived at the small inn a mile outside Geneva, where Kate had decided I should spend the night – she was staying at another hotel quite close, no doubt to the chagrin of André's parents – I found her in a state of considerable agitation. She was walking round and round her room, whispering, "What am I doing? Dare I do this?"

I sat quietly in the corner, near a high, shuttered window, watching one triumphant moonbeam play on the wooden floor. I knew silence at that moment was best.

"I'm going to do this . . . yes?"

"Yes, I think you are."

"Will it be OK?"

"Yes, it will be OK, Kate."

"It won't last . . . will it?"

"No."

"But it will help, for a time."

"I think so."

"He's nice, isn't he, Jack?"

"Yes, he's nice."

"Reasonably kind?"

"Reasonably."

"He's crazy about me."

"As they say."

"I'm sorry for him. I'm so sorry for him."

"He's getting you, Kate. Few people are sorry for him."

"Are you?"

"Yes . . . I'm sorry for him."

"He's pulling me to the surface."

"I know."

"I really will try to make him happy."

"I know you will."

She started to weep. And then:

"Can you hear that old music from the two of them? Can you still hear it?"

"No . . ."

"Please, Jack. I will try and stop thinking of them if you will please dance with me."

"No."

"Ah well. Ah well. I'll try to think of other things, Jack. Let's see. Tomorrow, a hairdresser is coming at nine to my hotel. After that, at about ten-thirty, a make-up girl will arrive to spend an hour touching and patting and blotting my face with little powder-dripping brushes and palettes of colour, so that I will look completely natural all day long. She's the best, and very expensive. She's a present from my agency. They've flown her in."

"That's very generous of them."

"They think I've a great future in the business." She laughed. Then suddenly, "Don't look at me today. Not closely."

"I won't."

"Will you give me something . . . to help me?"

"I thought you'd stopped."

"I have. But today is . . ."

"I can't, Kate."

She wept, again.

"Do you remember her tweed suits and her silk headscarves? And how tall he was? And his hair, his wonderful hair."

I stayed silent.

"Do you remember, Jack?"

"Not now, Kate."

"You're right."

Then she picked up a glass and held it up in a mock toast. "Here's to my newest, new beginning."

"To your newest, new beginning."

"Dance with me, Jack."

"No . . ."

"Please, Jack. Otherwise I might fall. I might sink."

I know the dangers here. Over the years however, to my mind's perception I have annexed a belief that I can circumvent them. I have engaged myself in a ritual, one that allows me to guide her over the abyss. But just as trapeze artists – high up on the tight-rope – judiciously place one foot before the other on the taut isthmus of hope on which they balance, I too proceed with great care. The number of times I, like them, have edged forward without precipitation, is irrelevant. The terror does not lessen. They, like me, carry on because they cannot stop. Like me, they cannot stop because to stop might prove fatal. Suspended lives are sometimes safer.

"Dance with me. Oh please, Jack, please."

And having paused for some time, in order to assure myself that nothing in that room could destabilize us, eventually, as always, I said,

"Yes."

And we danced.

And when we dance, as we rarely do, she takes her clothes off. As do I. And we fold them meticulously on chairs which we place facing each other on opposite sides of the room. Her chiselled, white hip-bone touches the outer muscles and skin of my thigh. Her arms are stiff and shop-mannequin-like, her right arm stretches across my chest. The fingers touch my shoulder, the left arm, taut, directioned, keeps the distance between us.

In whatever room we find ourselves, I first face the door and she the window. I am as familiar with her white breasts and golden pubic hair as she is with my penis, whether it is erect or not. These marks of gender are irrelevant for, as we dance, we neither truly touch nor see. I lead her towards the door, in perfect time to music we alone can hear, stepping backwards, as she follows me. When we reach the door we change about and, in a formal perfection, dance back to the window.

And that night I remember we danced, as other nights, in silence. I remember that the antique grandfather clock seemed to stand sentinel between the windows, as though fearful that we would forget time altogether. Slowly, the grey-white beginnings of the day added urgency to the low rhythm of the clock beating out its heart's desire that time be noted. They broke up the desiccated-grape-coloured night. Later, I knew they would fade away into the grey-mauve hues of the winter afternoon of her wedding day.

Finally, it was neither the time nor the light which stopped us. We simply fell, dry-eyed and dry-bodied, on the carpet. Then normal rhythms reasserted themselves and she got up and went to the bathroom and I heard the sounds of the shower and then the lavatory. When she returned to the room, without looking at me, she walked slowly towards her neatly folded clothes. As always, she stepped first into her knickers, then fastened her bra, pulled on her pale grey, hold-up stockings and, balancing on first one and then the other leg with ballerina-like precision, she placed her shoes on her long feet. Then she seemed to slither into a grey wool dress, and wrapping a giant shroud of red wool around her body, she left me without a word.

I remained still lying on the floor, thinking, perhaps too deeply, on the event.

Five

~

BY THE time I've tidied up after the unexpected invasions of this Saturday morning, I decide that for the rest of the day I will withdraw from the world and work on a lecture I've been invited to give next Tuesday, to a London conference of European psychiatrists. This invitation to join a number of other speakers, each of them more eminent than myself, was a direct result of my appearing on a Channel 4 discussion on the limitations of trauma counselling. This five-minute appearance drew unexpected praise from one of the great and the good in my profession, who must have presumably put my name forward to join Tuesday's panel. I scan the opening paragraphs on which I'd been working last week.

PSYCHIATRIC GREENE-LAND
The Politics of Doubt

AS ANY ARCHITECT WILL TELL YOU, TRAGEDY IMPROVES DESIGN. THERE WOULD SEEM, HOWEVER, TO BE LITTLE EVIDENCE THAT THE BENIGN AFTER-EFFECT OF CATASTROPHE, THAT OF IMPROVED SAFETY IN CONSTRUCTION, OR INDEED RECONSTRUCTION, APPLIES TO THE HUMAN PSYCHE.

WE DO NOT HAVE THE LUXURY, IF I MAY PUT IT LIKE THAT, OF GOING BACK TO THE DRAWING-BOARD. AND THE SUPREME ARCHITECT — I MEAN NO DISRESPECT —

SEEMS UNWILLING TO SCRAP THE DESIGN ENTIRELY AND TO START AGAIN FROM SCRATCH. WHICH LEADS TO A NUMBER OF, PERHAPS FROM ME, STRANGE QUESTIONS.

UNTIL 1850 THE SOLE NAME FOR WHAT WE WOULD CALL THE UNCONSCIOUS, WAS HELL, THE DEVIL'S TERRITORY. FORAYS INTO THE REGION WERE THEREFORE REGARDED AS COURTING DAMNATION. WE NOW KNOW MEMORY LIES IN THE LIMBIC SYSTEM, ONE OF THE DEEPEST AND OLDEST PARTS OF THE BRAIN, WHERE OUR PRIMITIVE DRIVES AND EMOTIONS ARE ALSO GENERATED. MY POST-FREUDIAN QUESTIONS THEREFORE ARE, HOW DEEP SHOULD WE GO IN EXAMINATION OF OUR SELVES AND OUR PAST? DO WE UNDERSTAND ITS DANGERS? THAT IT IS POSSIBLE TO DROWN IN THE *MOI PROFOND*? INDEED THAT IT IS POSSIBLE TO FALL AND VANISH INTO ONE'S PAST?

HAVE WE NOW BURDENED OUR PAST NOT ONLY WITH THE WEIGHT OF YEARS, BUT WITH THE EXPECTATION THAT IT SHOULD YIELD TO US THE VERY KEY TO THE PRESENT AND THE FUTURE? DO WE UNDERESTIMATE THE POWER OF AMBIGUITY, UNAWARE THAT THERE ARE DANGERS IN RESOLUTION? ARE WE SPENDING LARGE SWATHES OF TIME BANGING ON THE DOOR OF TIME PAST, WHICH IN TRUTH IS ALWAYS LOCKED AGAINST US?

OR, IS IT POSSIBLE THAT CREATIVE EXISTENTIALISM OR ELECTIVE *OMERTA* IS OUR BEST HOPE?

OUR RELATIONSHIP WITH OUR PAST IS, EVEN IN THE CONTEXT OF MATHEMATICS, A COMPLEX ONE. FOR EXAMPLE, THE YEARS ARE LIVED IN SINGLE FILE, BUT WE REMEMBER THEM IN CLUSTERS. THIS IS THE STRANGE CONSISTENCY OF NARRATIVE FORM THAT I HAVE LONG NOTED IN MY PATIENTS. EACH TELLS A STORY, A DRAMA, BUT THEY DO NOT START AT THE BEGINNING. MOST

START AT A POINT IN THEIR LIVES AT WHICH THEY ARE, IN A SENSE, ARRESTED. THEY SCRAMBLE THROUGH MEMORY OF THE BEFORE AND AFTER, PICKING SIGNS AND OMENS FROM A MIXED-UP JUMBLE OF YEARS — THE VOLUME OF THEIR PAST. SOME WONDER AT THE LIFE BEFORE IN WHICH THEY WERE NOT AS MUCH FULL OF HOPE AS FULL OF THE ASSUMPTION THAT, AS IT IS, SO IT WILL BE. OR THAT AT LEAST THE FUTURE WAS A PLACE WHERE THINGS WOULD BE RESOLVED. THEY NOW BEGIN TO PERCEIVE IT AS A PLACE WHERE THINGS WILL END.

IT MUST BE NOTED THAT EVEN THE ELEMENTS OF COMMUNICATION OF THAT PAST, i.e. CHOICE OF LANGUAGE AND VOCAL EMPHASIS, ARE THEMSELVES OPEN TO A MYRIAD INTERPRETATIONS. FOR WITHIN THE PRIVATE IMAGE WHICH WE APPLY TO WORDS LIES, OF COURSE, THE HIDDEN PICTORIAL REPRESENTATION OF THEIR INDIVIDUAL MEANING TO US.

THE WORD "LAKE" TO A MAN WHOSE CHILD HAS DROWNED NEVER CONJURES UP THE VISION OF "A LARGE SHEET OF WATER WITHIN LAND". THE WORD HAS LOST ITS INNOCENCE FOR HIM.

And the memory of Henry Purcell, dead now, stops me. He died of a broken heart though the death certificate said thrombosis. He was one of my first patients. He came to me five years after what he'd always referred to as "the tragedy". He never used the word "drowning", I remember that vividly. Henry Purcell was a gruff man, very awkward and eventually, if I'm truthful, unsavable. No. If I'm completely truthful, I couldn't save him. During that first year, something arrogant in me had crowded out with words the hushed, though alert, endurance, which I now believe essential to my work.

I return to my lecture, Henry Purcell's voice echoing in my mind.

OVER TIME I HAVE BECOME MORE SENSITIVE TO CERTAIN, OFTEN EXTREMELY SUBTLE CHANGES WHICH HIGHLIGHT, THE WAY A MARKER DOES ON TEXT, THE INHERENT TENSION IN THE SPEAKER WHICH MAKES A SPECIFIC WORD RESONATE WHEN SPOKEN. EVEN WHEN IT IS SPOKEN OUT OF THE CONTEXT OF SPECIFIC TRAGEDY.

THE THREAD OF THE VOICE, WHICH EMERGES FROM THE VERY DEPTHS OF OURSELVES, IS A POWERFUL GUIDE TO THE CHROMATIC RANGE OF OUR PASSIONS AND DESIRES. A FACT WHICH IS DAILY AUTHENTICATED BY MY PATIENTS. WE ARE AS MUCH DEFINED BY OUR VOCAL AS BY OUR VISUAL EXPRESSIONS AND THE VOICE IS THE MOST PERFECT SELF-PORTRAIT OF THE INNER SELF. IT IS THE GUIDE TO THE EMOTIONAL VOLTAGE OF LANGUAGE.

A RECENT STUDY AT YALE UNIVERSITY ESTABLISHED THAT A SUBTLE CHANGE IN THE SOUND OF THE VOICE IS THE FIRST SIGN THAT AN INDIVIDUAL MAY BE SERIOUS ABOUT COMMITTING SUICIDE. THE CHANGE IS SO DISTINCTIVE THAT PSYCHIATRISTS PLAN TO USE THE SOUND CHANGE AS AN EARLY-WARNING SYSTEM TO SEPARATE THOSE WHO ARE SERIOUSLY SUICIDAL FROM THOSE WHO ARE MERELY DEPRESSED. "IN SUICIDAL PATIENTS, THE VOICE BECOMES SLIGHTLY HOLLOW AND EMPTY, YOU GET THIS CHANGE IN QUALITY . . . IT IS CALLED THE VOICE FROM THE GRAVE," SAYS STEPHEN SILVERMAN, THE AUTHOR OF THE REPORT.

SO, THE LANGUAGE WE CHOOSE AND THE VOCAL EMPHASIS WE GIVE TO OUR CHOICE ILLUMINATE NOT WHAT HAPPENED, BUT OUR OWN COMPLEX REACTION TO THE MEMORY OF THAT EVENT. A MEMORY WHICH OVER

THE YEARS IS REINTERPRETED IN THE LIGHT OF NEW EVENTS. AUTHENTICITY IS THEREFORE MOST OFTEN A CHIMERA.

Who was it wrote, that to profoundly understand just one human being is the beginning of wisdom? A French novelist I think. I like to be able to quote widely and not just from textbooks. This tendency is what Ellie referred to as my Marcus Aurelius complex, after I'd been particularly pompous one evening. Perhaps she understood me better than I thought.

THE TRUTH OF A SINGLE HUMAN BEING'S EXPERIENCE MAY IN THE END BE IMPOSSIBLE TO ESTABLISH. IN MINING THE SPECIFIC ARCHAEOLOGY OF A HUMAN PSYCHE WE CAN ONLY GUESS AT THE TRUTH WITH THE TOOLS AVAILABLE TO US, i.e. THE KNOWLEDGE THEY HAVE SHARED WITH US AND OUR OWN MEAGRE CAPACITY FOR EMPATHETIC UNDERSTANDING.

AND YET, LADIES AND GENTLEMEN, THOUGH AWARE OF THESE INADEQUACIES I, LIKE YOU, HAVE CHOSEN TO SPEND MY LIFE IN THE FOLLOWING ENDEAVOUR:

Which is what, I ask myself?

THAT OF AIDING THE PATIENTS WHO COME TO ME — WHEN THE VERSION OF REALITY THAT WORKED PREVIOUSLY FOR THEM IS BREAKING DOWN — TO BE "EQUAL TO CIRCUMSTANCE". TO SOME THIS MAY SEEM A SMALL ACHIEVEMENT, BUT IT IS MY VERSION OF TRIUMPH.

As I open a bottle of water, I think that I sometimes see myself as the privileged observer of a multiplicity of privacies. An observer, but one who is expected to shape the view. With some of my patients, I try to help them to see their problems more clearly. There are others, whose problems are so starkly and irrefutably clear to them, and to me, that further clarity is their least requirement. Alternative perspectives do not apply to the death of a loved one. And facing it straight on, though essential, is agony. And after the agony? As I return to my computer I try to summarize what I know of the aftermath of grief.

GRIEF UNDERMINES THE INTELLECTUAL NAVIGATIONAL TOOLS OF THE CONSCIOUS MIND. FOR A TIME IT BECOMES NO MORE THAN A DORMITORY FOR THE DEAD. THE RESULT IS THE LOSS, SOMETIMES FATAL, OF DIRECTIONAL HOPE.

WHAT IS NEEDED, OVER TIME, IS A METHOD OF DISTANCING THEMSELVES SO THAT SOME FORM OF PERSPECTIVE MAY BE ACHIEVED. ONE WHICH WILL AT LEAST ALLOW LIFE IN A REASONABLE FORM TO CONTINUE.

I sip my water again and think of how irritated I become when I talk to people outside my rooms and find that the wounded lack compassion for the neurotic, whom they are convinced do not know what true suffering is. And that the neurotic sense a kind of right-wing brutalism in their condescension, if not contempt, for what they see as self-inflicted torture. Because we all experience others within ourselves, as they do us, each has very little sympathy with the other. And neither can comprehend the world of the clinically insane. Whom, beneath the clichéd sophisticated response, they still regard with almost medieval horror. There is com-petition, even in the suffering stakes. It can take a long time to lay down one's trophy. Shall I put this into the lecture? No. Too provocative. Let's try this.

THOUGH THERE IS USUALLY A HIDDEN INTERNAL CONSISTENCY IN EVEN THE MOST ERRATIC BEHAVIOUR, THERE IS OFTEN A MYSTERIOUS INCOMMENSURABILITY BETWEEN THE INNER AND THE OUTER LIFE; ONE TRAPPED WITHIN THE OTHER. BENEATH THE VISION OF THE HUMAN BODY IN ACTION AND CONCEALED SOMETIMES FROM THE PERSON THEMSELVES, LIES THE DETERMINANT INTERIOR. THE MASTER WHO PROVIDES MOTIVE FOR ALL WE SAY OR DO. A PEACEFUL COEXISTENCE BETWEEN THE TWO MARKS THE HARMONIOUS LIFE. AND WHEN THE BATTLE RAGES I AM SOMETIMES ABLE TO DETECT THE *CAUSUS BELLI* BUT ONLY SOMETIMES.

BECAUSE IT MAY BE IN THE STORY PEOPLE CHOOSE NOT TO TELL, THAT THEIR TRUE PERSONALITY LIES. NOT BECAUSE OF WHAT HAS NOT BEEN REVEALED, BUT BECAUSE *THIS* WAS THE SPECIFIC FACT THEY CHOSE TO HIDE. AND LIKE PHOSPHORUS, THAT SECRET, THE INNER SCRIPT WHICH THEY WILL TAKE TO THE GRAVE, GLEAMS WITH MAXIMUM INTENSITY WHEN IT IS ABOUT TO DIE . . .

Damn! I want to keep that phosphorus image but it's not working here. This whole thing is going to need hours of revision and tweaking. Why did I allow myself to be flattered into this?

My phone is ringing. Life is a series of bloody interruptions and someone is always calling us from somewhere. Though the direction of the call is often difficult to discern.

Just as I reach the receiver, the answerphone clicks in. The voice of the young woman I sleep with fills the room. It is clear that she is very angry with me. She loves me so much – when you don't seem to be getting that message from women, they turn the volume up. She is in a rage with me for breaking promises I never made, and for letting her down in circumstances in which I had never made any commitment to save her. I listen impassively to the notes of her anger and suffering, but in a sense I just can't bear the style in which she suffers.

The very tone of her voice is enough to make me determined that there are absolutely no circumstances in which I will ring her back today. Kindness is as often elicited by the presentation of anguish as by the anguish itself. And nowadays the careful exploitation of pain in order to maximize our compassionate response is virtually an art form.

At two o'clock I give up working on my lecture and go to the cinema, alone, *La Règle du jeu*. Programme notes in *Time Out* inform me that it enraged the critics when first shown. That Renoir left France in despair after its release. The film was "too superficial". It was "too frivolous", they said.

But then no one is ever thanked for reminding us that the dance continues and always will. Even if we have to step over dead bodies in order to keep time with the music.

Six

H AROLD ABST lives in Eaton Square. In London, little more needs to be known of a man's worldly position than his address. Indeed, until a short time ago, one could even guess political allegiance by postcode alone. However, since the left no longer requires financial sacrifice − contempt for the rich is *so unmodern* − where better to put one's extra cash than into property? A fine address, combined with a clear conscience, is delightful to behold and, in his own way, Harold, a member of London's *haute juiverie*, seems a charming man.

His family wealth, originally based on local newspapers, has been greatly increased by the judicious acquisition of specialist magazines. His company, which is currently pursuing a Stock Market flotation, is, I read last week, likely to be valued at £400 million. He has long been a Labour supporter, speaking out through his papers against the privatization of public utilities and the disgraceful condition of schools in the catchment areas of his various local papers.

Alas, for Harold's children, a daily journey from Eaton Square to one such school would have presented serious logistical problems. Therefore, although they were exactly the kind of family who could have effected change in the situation, his children, when young, were forced to forgo the joys inherent in the satisfying feeling that their civic duty had been done. Instead they morally slummed it at Lady Eaton's and Hill House.

In the mid-1990s, as the prospect of a Labour victory looked ever more certain, his generosity to the cause increased dramatically. Harold does not, I gather, like to waste his money. There were continuing rumours of a peerage. This honour, should it come his way, will almost certainly be based on his work for an Inner London hospital charity appeal. All this I'd gleaned during a rather uncomfortable *Newsnight* investigation of the honours system about a year or so ago, when Kate had first started seeing Harold Abst. He was one of four men on the panel, and made it crystal-clear that were he ever to be offered a peerage, he would only accept in order to see the current House overthrown. This philosophy was hugely popular at the time with those who were consumed with a hatred of power and privilege, unless the power and privilege were theirs. The peerage has not as yet arrived; a postponement rather than a cancellation. Since the hereditary principle has already been abolished, on his eventual elevation to the House Harold's energies need not be wasted on this issue.

These are the innocent hypocrisies of the world and merit little in the way of condemnation. Harold has played an old game and played it well. His success simply demonstrates a determined, worldly intelligence. Which makes me a little apprehensive as I press the bell to his apartment.

The butler opens the door and leads me to the drawing-room. Harold is alone. He rises to greet me.

"Jack, I really appreciate this. Kate's upstairs, dressing. You know I wish she would move in here permanently but she still wants to keep her old flat."

"I know."

I take the proffered drink and sit down on the sofa

opposite his, trying not to disturb the cushions which, like a regiment of soldiers, stand to attention on it. On the wall opposite me, an unyielding Francis Bacon figure seems in warrior-like opposition to a Matisse *jeune fille*. I feel in some strange way that the paintings add to the suppressed feeling of tension between Harold and myself. We look at each other for a few minutes, in an increasingly uncomfortable silence. Harold, a man of action, rises suddenly and says:

"Shall we go to my study? We've got half an hour before anyone is expected."

I follow his rather heavy, imposing figure down the red-carpeted hall. He takes a key from his pocket and opens the door. I think how surprising it is that he should keep his study locked. Then I remind myself that I lock my consulting-rooms every time I leave them.

His study is not at all what I had expected. I suppose I had imagined something more conventional; a dark leather-bound desk perhaps, heavy chairs, a carpet. In fact, the room is uncarpeted. On a polished wooden floor a vast slate table has been placed in front of, though some distance from, an Elizabethan fireplace. A high-backed chair, upholstered slightly more conventionally in an Aubusson pattern, is positioned on the fireplace-side of the table; perhaps on the principle that his back is thus more protected.

There are no computers or whirring fax machines, nor indeed any sign of what I thought would be the essential tools of the businessman's life. As though he reads my mind, he signals to a small door at the other end of the room.

"I keep all the other stuff in a little ante-room just off this one. I come in here to think and to read."

The tall windows, which look out on to the square, have dark, chocolate-coloured silk curtains. They billow slightly at the top, like an Edwardian lady's bosom, and are held, as though embraced at the waist, by thick, braided ropes. Their skirts virtually rustle on the floor. The garden square, on to which the windows allow Harold Abst to gaze while contemplating his life, is a manicured perfection. It is London living, but not as most people know it.

The wall opposite the windows is covered, floor to ceiling, with bookshelves. I glimpse a number of slim volumes of poetry. On the small side-table, by the chair into which he motions me, novels by Mishima and Kawabata are stacked. *Beauty and Sadness* lies open, as though the reader had been interrupted suddenly.

He notices me looking at the books.

"Have you read Kawabata?"

"No."

"You should. Less lurid than Mishima but ultimately more chilling. He understands the subtleties and cruelties involved in love. He is, in my opinion, the master of female erotic psychology. He gassed himself. I'm sure there's no connection between the two."

"Why such an interest in Japanese literature?" I ask him. An interest, in the light of what he's just said, that I find faintly chilling.

"I spent two years in Tokyo. Just after university, when I wasn't really certain whether I wanted to take over my father's business or not. Even in that short time it was possible to note the tension between *The Chrysanthemum and The Sword,* do you know that book?"

I shake my head. This is not as I had imagined.

"Add it to your list. Better still, I'll send it to you. That tension is not only part of their culture, but of all human relationships. A fact of which I'm sure you're well aware."

We look at each other. And again, the silence is less than companionable.

"They're good on despair as well. 'The special quality of Hell is to see everything clearly down to the last detail. And to see all that in the darkness.' Great line, don't you think?" Harold expects confirmation.

"Yes."

Silence. Perhaps I should have sounded more enthusiastic?

"She's not a happy woman, your sister."

"Really?"

He smiles. "Yes, really. I've been married twice and had many . . ."

". . . Liaisons?"

"Lovers," he replies crisply, as though he finds the word "liaisons" childish. "I was engaged to someone else before I met Kate," he continues.

"That's a quaint phrase when you're contemplating a third marriage." I feel the need to get my own back in this game of sexual semantics.

"Quite. But her family is conventional and she had never been married before. A virgin, so to speak, in marital terms." He smiles again and continues; "She was very, very angry when I told her about Kate. Very angry indeed. As were her family. A Scots father spitting rage is to be avoided at all costs."

"I'll remember that."

"Do. It's good advice."

"Where is she now?"

"I settled some money on her. She's travelling. First class, of course. Her father, I gather, is absolutely astonished that she made so much from the sale of her little boutique that she is able to travel so extensively."

"I'm sure he is."

"I'm telling you this little tale to emphasize the degree to which Kate has disturbed my life. And to indicate how serious I am about her."

"I rather assumed you were serious. Since I gather you intend marrying her."

"I've found that you can marry, be in love even, without being deeply serious about someone."

"I didn't know that, Harold."

"Oh, I think you did. There are other duties, of course, in my life. My commitment to a number of Jewish charities. Did you know that here in England we have the fastest-declining Jewish community in the world? I say this as a man who has married out twice and is contemplating doing so a third time. Hypocrisy, perhaps?"

"No, not at all."

"I'm also deeply committed to the Labour Party. I'm aware of their failings, but I prefer their rhetoric. It is at least important to state aims that are worthy, don't you think?"

I nod vaguely.

"You regard that as easy virtue, do you?" he asks.

"A luxury, perhaps. One we did not win."

"Ah. That heroic, resented generation . . ."

And I think how now we strive to be our best selves, while doing everything possible to avoid the pain involved.

"Resented? Yes, I think you're right," I reply, and feel a sudden bond between us. I doubt that it will last.

"Apart from these commitments," he says, returning to

his theme, "I've been serious, deadly serious, about only one other thing in my life – money. What the Americans call the almighty dollar. They see money as a moral force. Which is why they work much harder than we do incidentally. Twenty-four seven, as they say now."

"Twenty-four seven?"

"Twenty-four hours a day, seven days a week. And, may I say, with few incidents of Karoshi."

"Karoshi?" What the hell is he talking about?

"Death from overwork. The curse of the Japanese at the moment. A friend of mine was telling me the other day that platform mirrors have been installed in railway stations in Tokyo in the hope of deterring the would-be suicide. I don't expect their appearance on Grand Central Station, at least not in the near future. Americans pursue money without guilt. They revere it, they cultivate and they harvest it. In England, individual conscience confuses everyone. The law protects the businessman in America. Within the system he can be very tough. An accumulation of wealth, therefore, is like an accumulation of good deeds to set before God on the Day of Judgement. Like farmers praying for rain, they pray for markets."

"Have you ever prayed for markets?"

"I am not a religious man, Jack."

I sense that we're off the subject of money.

"May I come to the point? I am aware of how much Kate relies on your judgement. Naturally, therefore, I wish to paint myself in as favourable a light as possible. I would guess that the best way to do that with you, Jack, is to be honest about my less than perfect past.

"I'm over fifty. Fifty-two to be exact. I have had two wives. I have three children. I confess to being rather surprised by these facts of my life. The role of stepmother will not be onerous. My eldest children, twins, twenty-two, live in New York with their mother, Susan. She's married to a hugely successful banker and has just been elevated to the Hall of Fame of Best Dressed Women. It's an elevation that she seems to equate with winning the Nobel Peace Prize, and, alas, amongst her circle, is probably just as revered. She adored me when we married. Then . . . well . . . you know how these things go."

I murmur assent. It is clearly an adequate response, for he continues, "My youngest son, Carlo, sixteen, lives with his mother in Rome. When things become intolerable for him he comes here, school permitting. He is at what I call the Sonny-von-Bulow stage with his mother. He loves her, of course, but wishes she lay in a coma-like state unable to move and, most particularly, unable to talk. His entire relationship with her would be limited to weekly visits to her bedside. Naturally he would bring flowers. Carlo will find Kate's quiet, not to say almost silent, demeanour attractive. As I do."

"Look, Harold, I'm slightly puzzled by all this. I mean . . . Kate's over thirty. She'll come to her own decision, which, for what it's worth, I think will be yes. Personally, I'd be very pleased if she remarried and, again for what it's worth, I think you'll be very good for her."

He gets up, clearly angry at being patronized, as he no doubt sees it, and walks across to his desk. As he stands there the iconic power of a desk, its ability to hierarchically discriminate, strikes me again. I never, ever, speak to anyone from the opposite side of a desk.

He sits behind the desk and, turning his face slightly away from me, looking towards the windows, begins to speak.

"I sometimes get up at night and sit here. There is a

street-light just outside so I rarely draw the curtains. I like to hear the muted sound of traffic and to listen to the cars as they turn into and then out of the Square. This is where I sit and think of Kate. And sometimes I study these objects . . ."

He motions to a formal-looking composition of ornaments on the table.

". . . And remember what has gone before and where exactly on my journey Kate joins me. Do you see that arrangement on my desk? You'll probably consider it strange for a businessman's desk. Your interpretation would be interesting. Perhaps . . . sometime in the future . . ."

I look down at a black, iron cat playing with a dark red ball, beside which is a sculpture of a child's hand. An ivory fan, locked, has been placed in the exact centre, a position that seems almost incongruously aggressive for an object associated with gentleness. A miniature printing plate, two wedding rings placed meticulously side by side, and three exquisitely carved jade boxes complete the arrangement.

"The black cat was one of the few things my father took with him when he left Russia. I won't bore you with the immigrant's tale, except to say that neither my family nor I are where Fate once decreed we should be. Which is, of course, just what Fate also decreed.

"The sculpture of a child's hand is that of my brother, who died when he was three. My mother never spoke of it. So I do understand certain silences. Do you know Wittgenstein? *Whereof one cannot speak thereof one must be silent.*

"And this is my mother's fan. Locked. The significance won't be lost on you. The printing plate is from the first edition of the first paper my father launched in this country. With a loan from his father-in-law."

He pauses, glances at the wedding rings and to my relief, makes no reference either to them or to the three jade boxes. Then he stands up suddenly and says, "I have become enchanted by Kate." He turns away from me for a moment, carefully unlocks a drawer in a cabinet behind him and takes out a copy of a glossy magazine. I cannot quite read his expression as he hands it to me.

"Do you remember this?"

I look at it and shake my head.

"It's about eight years old. It contains an interview which she gave during the early days of her marriage to Bronfman. Page 40, I think you'll find."

As I leaf through, trying to find page 40, not easy with unnumbered advertising pages, he continues:

"I kept it chiefly for the photograph."

And there she was. Standing on a rock, precariously balanced above a mistral-whipped Mediterranean, wearing a red, strapless ballgown. She was looking over her shoulder, her back to the camera. Her hair, in complete contrast to the formality of the dress, seemed to billow out above her right shoulder, like a shawl. Her face was flushed, whether by the sun or by make-up, I've no idea. The caption on the facing page reads:

A Rosy Redhead, A Racing Riva, And Me,
Your Rubicund Reporter,
Bill Secher

And I remember that during her honeymoon she had stayed at the new hotel her then parents-in-law had just built outside St. Tropez. I suppose as part of a publicity drive for the venture, she had co-operated with the article. It was all innocent enough. The reporter, though predictably mocking various aspects of the young couple's spoiled life, was nevertheless, if I remember correctly, quite taken with Kate.

"Go to the last paragraphs."

I do as instructed and read . . .

Kate Harrington entered our lives as The Walking Girl, *the video artwork that was the first work of the artist Joshua Prendergast. This fifteen-minute vision of the silent Kate Harrington walking through a seemingly endless series of doors, was mesmeric, as much because of Harrington's strange beauty as the artist's conceptualisation. She worked with Prendergast (whose determination to overcome the disadvantages of his background – aristocratic – and his education – Eton and Cambridge – resulted in him becoming one of the great unwashed, dressed exclusively in Oxfam rejects) on a number of experimental films. These led to her being picked by* Arbus *to launch its perfume,* Mona Lisa. *She was dropped by them a year later, when in an interview she'd quoted Pater on the Mona Lisa describing her as one "who has learned the secrets of the grave". Harrington was, as usual, evasive when I questioned her about the break-up of her relationship with Prendergast, who is known to say, with some bitterness on the subject, "The walking girl walked".*

Now she is Mrs. André Bronfman, one of our most beautiful models who is also a clever girl with a degree from Cambridge. A modern miss who says she wants to concentrate on helping her husband's business and will therefore probably give up her career shortly. A young married woman who shies away from the question of children. In a sense, Kate Harrington is an aberration. She doesn't seem to fit into any pattern.

Anyway, what do I know? All I want is to have enough money to withdraw from the world for a year to write an award-winning novel. This personal ambition is shared with you, dear reader, in order to make it clear that I could have been eaten alive with jealousy. Instead, well, the girl is unforgettable. So, good on ya, Kate. My wife's Australian.

I put the magazine down on the slate table. He looks at it for a moment, then carefully locks it away in the drawer again. He glances at his watch, and says, "We've got a while yet. I know Kate's not in love with me. Not that it makes a lot of difference in a marriage. As I said, my first wife adored me. I was twenty-six; it seemed incredibly important at the time to be adored. Youth, no doubt."

"No doubt." I hope my tone is not too sarcastic.

There is a slight note of impatience as he says, "I'm wondering why you ask so few questions of the man your sister is contemplating marrying."

"I was under the impression you wished to ask me questions."

"Very well then. I had hoped we could be more subtle. Let me ask you straight out . . . why does Kate say so little about her background?"

Hesitation is fatal. The words come immediately.

"There is very little to tell. Our mother died when we were young and our father, who lives in America, and with whom we lost contact years ago, found it impossible to cope. We were brought up in Harley Street, by Dr. Edmund Harrington, my grandfather's half-brother, who was our closest and most suitable relative."

"Wasn't he rather old to take on two children?"

"There was a fifteen-year age-gap between Edmund

and my grandfather. The second marriage didn't work out and Edmund's mother left Ireland and returned with him to England. Edmund became a doctor, then a consultant cardiologist, and set up his practice in the house in which I now work and live, which he generously left to us. I bought Kate out when she got married. Edmund also managed, with great care, certain monies from the sale of the house and land in Ireland. I honestly can't think of anything else to tell you." I have concentrated on various financial details in order to distract him from more intrusive questions.

"Hmm. I can see how alike you two are. I didn't think so when I first met you. The romance of Kate's past is fascinating to me. She's once or twice mentioned the house in which you were brought up, Mala . . . something. I understand the stubborn power of even the haziest child-hood memory of the house where one was born. I used to have a dream of a house in the country outside St. Petersburg, which my father had shown me once in a photograph. I played with the idea of returning in the post-*Glasnost* period and buying it, for holidays, short visits . . ."

I don't miss a beat.

"Oh, I think dreams of home for Kate and me are con-centrated in Harley Street. Edmund gave us a very good life."

"How very kind of Edmund," he says. "I'm sorry I never got a chance to meet him."

He glances at me. I look steadily back at him.

"Yes, it's a pity. You two would have got on very well."

"Thank you, Jack. Well, we'd better go in. It's a small dinner party, only ten people. Kenneth Deacon, the writer. Do you know him?"

"I've heard of him."

"His wife is Vanessa Crichton. She's in the BBC. Quite what she does there I've no idea. Then there's Walter MacIntyre and his wife. He's in the Justice Department in Washington. She's a brilliant banker. Also an old publishing friend of mine and his new wife, his third I think, whom I've never met. Your date is Alexa Richards, a very ambitious young actress. I gather your ex-wife was in the theatre. I feel inordinately proud to have gleaned that little nugget of information."

I am well aware from whom he got the "little nugget of information" but I say nothing. After a moment he continues:

"You Harringtons are hard going when it comes to facts."

"Perhaps because the facts of a life have so little to do with anything."

"What a shocking thought! Perhaps we can discuss the implications over dinner. And now, as my first wife used to say, it's show time . . ."

Seven

All dinner parties are theatrical by nature. The set is the dining-room. The best set, as Ellie told me, is a metaphor for the play. After a stint at the National as assistant director, Ellie made her name in a tiny theatre, alas long since closed, with a stunning production of Zola's *Thérèse Raquin,* which had been adapted for the stage by a brilliant young friend of hers who later committed suicide.

In her production, the body of the murdered husband, Camille, was displayed virtually nailed to the backdrop, so that the audience, like the haunted lovers and the paralysed mother, could never escape from his lingering, presumably putrefying, corpse. This directorial inspiration made her the absolute darling of the more avant-garde critics. My marriage to Ellie provided a crash course in theatre, for which I am grateful. But then the education one gains in marriage is rarely limited to the sexual and sentimental.

The set tonight is cardinal-red. Did Harold make this decision, or the previous owners? Who was it told me that Matisse's *Harmony in Red* was originally painted in blue and then painted over to intensify and enhance emotion? Were Ellie here tonight, it's possible she would judge the cardinal-red wallpaper and mahogany table gleaming with Sèvres, finely wrought silver candelabra and antique Lalique glass – I have Rose to thank for my ability to catalogue the table arrangement – as the perfect set for either a vicious high-society *Hedda Gabler,* or a modern version of Congreve's *The Way of the World.*

The giant white linen napkins – you can always tell a man by the size of his napkins, Rose again – spread out their folds in a starchy embrace as the first course, *quenelles* of sole garnished with pastry flowers, arrives. I feel as if I am in costume, but remain confused and uneasy about my lines.

Kate is at one end of the table, the one further from me, and Harold faces her at the other. Kate's performance tonight is astonishing. Gone is the woman who some hours ago was "sinking". Gone is the note in her voice which only I know. And which I fear, when her questions reach me from afar, in time not space. Gone too is a certain rhythm she uses, in those occasional middle-of-the-night calls which always begin:

"Jack, help me, Jack. Talk to me."

Which is not, of course, what she wants at all.

"What happened, Jack? What happened?"

And I tell her what she wants to hear. "You know, Kate. You know what happened."

And then she sighs, and says:

"Yes. I know. Ah well . . ."

And then, more quietly, she asks me, "Will we dance again soon, Jack?"

And I, in full knowledge of what it is that I do, always say, "Yes, soon."

And it's over. Sometimes for as long as a year. The answers she elicits and which through the years remain the same, are essential to her. She documents herself upon them.

Her voice tonight when she speaks, which is not very

often, is low and confident. Listening to her you could even say she sounds happy. She is almost the perfect hostess, attentive, welcoming and charming. I wonder if Kate is aware of how much she owes to Arnold Kessler, the man with whom she lived – in her version of "living with" – after her first marriage ended? Kate's way of living with someone includes regular escapes to South Street, the small flat she acquired with the money I paid her for her share of Harley Street. Shortly after Edmund died she married André. The purchase of the flat should have been a warning to him. But by then André was incapacitated by love and his instincts towards self-preservation had deserted him.

She didn't set out to bewitch Kessler, a notorious womanizer, who, when I spent a weekend with them, couldn't seem to enter a room without wishing to rearrange it, or see a woman without wishing to redesign her. But if she had, she couldn't have done better than her continued arbitrary disappearances to South Street. It took him a long time to understand that this was not a game of sexual politics. When his repeated proposals were rejected, he quickly married an impeccable young French woman of the *bon chic, bon genre*, school of female allure.

Kate told me that his mother, in an ecstasy of gratitude, signed over to him a large portion of her stock in the family company. But then mothers are always more interested in whom their sons marry than in whom their daughters choose. They know where power truly lies in a marriage and defeat by a daughter-in-law is particularly bitter.

During her years with Kessler, Kate learned the rules of the game. Rules which she is applying so expertly here tonight. In his house in Gloucestershire, where he'd liked to entertain, she'd agonized over the exact placement of those who *were* running the country and those who now are, of the media baron and his infuriatingly better-known columnist. She even gave serious consideration to how to mingle the currently happy and the currently sad. Each seemingly unaware that their state was temporary.

She learned how to maintain a balance of guests between business and politics and the distrusted observer of both, the media. And where to sprinkle the one or two lucky bastards who were artists, as Stoppard puts it, and the enraged academic, cleverer than all of them, but astonished to find that school's over.

She absorbed the disciplines of the *maîtresse de maison*. And, by the end of the relationship, she was able to weave her way through staff warfare like a general. She knew that those under her command marched best on a good, though not excessive, wage packet – they wonder *why* you're paying over the odds – much free time and an agreed, acceptable level of sulking.

Her appearance tonight is, as always, remarkable. She has the look of a woman who is used to being looked at. She is a woman who is aware that at whatever angle she holds her head, her profile will please, and for some do more than please. It will enchant. There is something inescapable about the power of this unmerited gift. For some time to come, there is nothing she or anyone else can do about it. Indeed, nothing other than an act of physical vandalism will detract from the pleasure Kate gives to anyone who looks at her. She is a work of art. Old school. She is wearing a long cream dress, whose drama lies in the way it falls almost to her waist at the back. A fact of which we were all aware as we followed her Helen-of-Troy-like figure from the sitting-room to the dining-room.

Alexa Richards, seated on my right, is a bright-poppy kind of girl. Jet-black hair, red lipstick that matches, as far as I can tell, the dramatic dress she is wearing. Alas, as she explains to me, this particular set, with its cardinal-red, does not match the dress.

"This is a lesson. Next time I'm not going to ring to find out whether it's long or short. I'm going to ask, what colour's your dining-room?"

Her laugh has a child's quality to it. And her bright little face looks questioningly at mine. Am I going to play the dinner-party game or not, it seems to ask? Of course I am. What kind of man do you think I am? And I'm off.

"Do you have a multi-coloured wardrobe, then?"

"No. Can't afford it. But in future, if I find out that it's an orange or a fuchsia-pink dining-room, I've got my two old friends, little black numbers from Valentino and Saint Laurent. My husband bought them for me. He was in the first flush of love. The dresses stayed the course. He didn't."

"Have you been separated long?"

"We're divorced. I think I may be coming up to my divorce anniversary. My mother reminded me of the date, in that thoughtful way mothers do. Every anniversary noted."

"An almanac of all our days."

"That sounds like the title of something or other. My ex-husband's a writer. Henry Ash . . . You needn't be embarrassed if you've never heard of him. He's not as famous as . . ." She nods conspiratorially to the famous author, whose name I can't now remember and who is seated at the far end of the table, on Kate's left.

". . . But he does a lot of rather good journalism. It's a curse to be talented when what you long for is genius. Do you think it's cruel of me to say he is definitely not a genius? If he hadn't been such an ambitious novelist, I think we'd still be together. You see, he succumbed to what I call the domino principle of divorce. It's a particularly lethal syndrome for writers."

"Why?"

"If one author divorces in their group, they don't commiserate, they envy him the experience. All that pain and anguish, for God's sake. The guy might write a Booker-nominated novel based on the *Sturm und Drang* of the break-up. *Littérature vérité*. Art has always demanded sacrifice so that first wife just has to go. Adultery's a speedy way out. Poor Henry. Since we didn't have children he was denied the bonus of experiencing that particular kind of wreckage first hand. Which was why, no doubt, the book wasn't terribly good. Next time he might be luckier."

"Next time?"

"Yes. He's a father now. He says he's besotted, of course. But I saw him the other day in the supermarket and he looked satisfyingly fed-up and totally exhausted. If any of his contemporaries embark on a second divorce, leaving both wailing wives and children, it will be curtains for . . . Oh God, I've forgotten her name." She laughs. And miraculously she sounds genuinely amused rather than angry. Then I remember she is an actress.

"Mind you," she continues, "even if they survive as a couple, she's going to have to adjust to life in the Big Apple. And on not very much money. My darling ex-husband has, I read in last week's paper, decided to leave England. The reason, as far as I could discern, is that alas England simply hasn't listened to him. We have not mended the errors of our ways, which he has so thoughtfully pointed out to us. Our sins are numerous, unspeakable, and took up three-quarters of the page. A very short paragraph was dedicated to America's more minor difficulties, like, for example, the death penalty, the gun lobby, lack of medical care for the poor. Peccadilloes like that. Anyway, he's just one of a group. Middle-aged wannabes who wannabe American. I'm longing to read a piece by him in a few months' time which might bravely deal with the historical exploitation of the native American Indian, how there's still a No Jews rule in some of the most expensive real estate in New York . . ."

She has decided to wound because she has been wounded. It's an old equation. Mind you, she might be right about the precariousness of her ex-husband's new relationship if he exiles himself to New York. Leaving once, and you only ever leave once, prepares you for other departures. I decide to change the subject.

"I know one is not supposed to ask, but are you in anything at the moment?"

It sounds so bloody awkward and I can't understand why I'm making such an effort. Maybe not to let Kate down, or to please Harold Abst. Which is, I suppose, the same thing. Alexa Richards is chirpily bitter. But she's bitter all the same. Then, why shouldn't she be?

"I'm thrilled you asked. If you hadn't, I'd have brought it into the conversation somehow. I'm rehearsing Annabella in '*Tis Pity She's a Whore*. Don't you just love that title?"

Harold is looking at me and smiling. Alexa Richards lowers her eyelids slowly.

"Has Jack told you his first wife is in the theatre?" Harold asks.

God, he's a tricky man. But maybe that's good for Kate.

"His first wife?"

Poppy Bright subjects me to the full force of her actress eyes, which are brimming with an expression of surprise. It must seem to her a vexing little evasion that I had not mentioned my connection to the world of theatre, however tangential it might be. Or perhaps – do I flatter myself here – because of the mention of another woman?

"Yes, Ellie my first wife, she's a director."

It is an eccentricity of which I am well aware, to refer to Ellie as "my first wife", rather than "my ex-wife". It doesn't take a genius to work out why.

"How many do you have?"

I'm inordinately pleased that she is still smiling at me.

"I can only boast of one."

"Time will cure that." Harold again. He is having a minor revenge. My aloof behaviour must have irritated him earlier. He is a man who likes to be in charge. To whom others must bow their will. For their own good, as he would see it. But there is always collusion in these matters.

The second course arrives. Sliced duck, served pink, nestles on a rainbow bed of mange-touts, carrots, water chestnuts and saffron rice. A beaming Harold tells us that the red wine is a Pomerol, *Château Petrus* 1978.

"I regard drinking anything bottled after 1982 as infanticide," he adds.

There's general laughter.

"Not my line, I'm afraid, though I'd love to claim it. But one must always attribute, don't you think, Kenneth?"

Harold smiles benignly down the table at Kenneth, who, though he looks slightly abashed, agrees whole-heartedly.

"That's a bit naughty of Harold. Kenneth Deacon was involved in a plagiarism case a short time ago," Poppy Bright says, in a low conspiratorial voice.

Harold may have made his remark in an innocent tone of voice; none the less what he said was clearly provocative, and to a guest. Perhaps Mr. Deacon has been flirting with Kate, or perhaps Harold is the kind of man who feels it necessary subtly to establish moral superiority. I have no more time to consider this issue. The silent sergeant-major of the dinner table has decreed "eyes left" and, obeying orders, I turn to the wife of the Justice Department lawyer, Joan.

"Do you enjoy living in Washington?"

Oh, the saving graces of the geographical-location conversation. The ultimate innocent question.

"Yes," she replies. "Though it's a one-topic town. Now we're back to politics. Mr. Clinton is to be congratulated for at least broadening the agenda. For a while it was possible to have an in-depth conversation on the theological implications of oral sex, without hysteria breaking out amongst the guests. That shift in the culture may be his most lasting legacy."

Harold leans over towards me and says, "Joan is a doctor of philosophy who became a merchant banker. A few years ago, she gave me the best advice of my business career. Never fall out with your finance director! Joan's the cleverest woman I know. Mind you, the world is full of clever women and they're running everything now."

"I hardly run the bank, Harold." She says this in a tone of voice which implies that she could, if only she wanted to.

"What exactly do you do there?"

"I try to persuade people to pay millions of dollars for

a company that makes no profit. Indeed, I persuade them that the greater the loss the company is making, the better investment it is likely to be."

"You can't be serious?"

"Deadly serious. It's getting very much harder than it was a couple of years ago. The new economy remains the promised land, but rather too much faith is required of those who demand proof of its existence every six months. If Nasdaq finally collapses, as God knows it threatens to, we're finished. So we're all talking it up. Do you know how overextended we are?"

"But shouldn't that be a reason to be more cautious?"

She laughs. "Ah, the innocence of the boy! Fees for investment banks are based on high valuation because we get a percentage of the total. The higher the price, the larger our fees, etc., etc. Naturally, we give objective advice."

"Isn't it a long journey from philosophy to money?" I ask her.

"Not as long as you think. Money genuinely fascinates me. Those who make billions, literally billions, at the moment, are in fact extraordinarily creative. They have a kind of musical genius. They pluck chords out of the air and play the right tune just at the right moment. It's the playing of the tune they enjoy, not the actual end-result, which is really just applause to them. I've known people who eight years ago were making $100,000 and are now worth billions."

"Not in England."

"Don't be bitter, Harold! Your lot go from £50,000 to many millions. Not so terrible. But I agree with you about America, which in the last eight years has made more money than any society in history. It's increasingly difficult for some multi-billionaires to know what on earth to do with their money. Eccentricity abounds. For example, I have a client who finds the chirping of the birds in the morning on his Mediterranean estate absolutely maddening. He has therefore sent out an order, 'Shoot the birds'. There is a small team at the moment especially employed for this purpose . . . Anyway, enough of all this financial talk. What did you think of the new show at Tate Modern?"

To my humiliation, I have to admit that I haven't seen it. There is a moment's silence while we search for another subject. Things are becoming slightly more heated as the wife of the famous author – didn't Harold say she was at the BBC? – launches a lethal attack on Tory arts sponsorship – or lack of – during those long-ago ghastly years of Tory power. Which had, according to Vanessa Crichton, totally wrecked, yes wrecked, the entire culture of this country. Poppy Bright whispers to me:

"She's the producer of . . ." and mentions a well-known soap opera which had come in for much newspaper criticism in the past week, but for reasons I couldn't quite remember.

The American lawyer rather bravely comments that current social third-degree in England is limited to "Are you now, or have you ever been, a member of the Conservative Party?" He says this with such grace that the provocative nature of the comment is drowned in grateful laughter.

The evening winds down eventually and I find myself standing on the steps contemplating a shared taxi with Poppy Bright. She looks a trifle disappointed – am I mis-reading this? – when she is scooped up by the American couple who have been informed by Harold that they pass "right by" her flat. She departs in their chauffeur-driven car, as I stand on the pavement, not looking, I hope, too forlorn. I am aware that I've been gently out-manoeuvred by Harold, but slightly too befuddled by wine to work out why.

Sitting in the taxi on the way home I wonder what, if anything, I gain from the mixture of truth and snare, the equivocal and mocking view of life, which a smart London dinner party affords. Whether the subject was the sexual mores of our time or the deadly game of modern finance, or Art, with a capital A, waves of speech had flowed over me. Passionless engagement which ended with a good brandy. It's a circuit, a lifeline to some – couples who must be out with a group every night in order to avoid murdering each other, or lonely singles whose despair can be drowned in the endless din of "darling". People rarely go to dinner just for the pleasure of food and wine, knowing that food and wine cannot compensate for other hungers.

It's Kate's life-raft. One she believes she needs. She certainly likes that life. She understands its disciplines, its constraints, which, though fierce in their own way, soothe her. But the disciplines of "the world" don't serve the creative impulse for Kate as they did for Eliot during his time as a banker or Larkin and Borges in their respective libraries – I waxed quite lyrical about this once in an essay on order and the creative mind. No, this life she leads roots Kate's mind firmly in the superficial, a more tenacious soil than one may think.

Society spins round and round forever, unstoppable, on its axis. Barely pausing when one of its members, however treasured, falls off – a Malthusian necessity – so that crowded society is never tested to the point of destruction, as though some ancient law from the Cabbala protected it. It regularly refreshes itself with new blood. But what the happy newcomer discerns as arrival at a static point, the top, is in fact nothing more than his temporary mounting of a fairground horse on a merry-go-round. It is his turn and whether he falls off or, stiff-jointed, dismounts, others are already gathering on the ground. Greedily they watch the spinning wheel of colour, listen to the laughter and the shrieks which they hope are of pleasure, desperately searching for a riderless horse to leap into sight.

Which, I hope, for some time at least, will not be Kate's.

Eight

———

SHE RINGS at about seven – from her flat. I wonder how Harold is adjusting to all this uncertainty. Like a patient fisherman, I would think, he can sense he's going to reel her in.

"Well, how did it go with Harold? Wake up, big brother. How did your conversation with Harold turn out?"

She's happy. That jocular tone, the rarely used sobriquet "big brother", mean she's happy.

"It went OK. He's very serious about you."

"I think I'm going to marry him. I honestly think I can make this work. I like the fact that he's been married twice. Is that stupid?"

"Well, it certainly shows experience."

"He's not like André. I won't break his heart. André was too much in love with me. It terrified me. You understand . . . that terror."

We neither of us speak for a few minutes. I lie back against the pillows and close my eyes. Eventually she says, "Oh God, Jack. What happened, Jack?"

"Not now, Kate. Not now."

She stops immediately.

"OK. To the future," she says.

And we consider the future. For some, it's the most attractive of the three phases of time.

"He wants to make a firm date for the wedding. I'm

going to say as soon as he wants. Just like that. Impressed? You must admit it's forward planning."

"I'm impressed."

"Be fair. At least I'm trying. Where was I?"

"About to get married."

She laughs. It's wonderful.

"We'll just do it. Quietly. Have a little party afterwards. It's all clear to him? I hate being questioned. You explained things to him, didn't you, Jack?"

"It's as clear as it's ever going to be. He's got the absolute truth; Mother being dead and the fact that we have no contact with Father; Edmund's adoption of us. How kind and generous he was to us. The rest, André and Kessler, he knows from you. I doubt he cares that you don't want children. He has three already."

"He says it's up to me."

"Good."

We pause. Decide to go no further.

"I must go," she says. "I needed to collect some things. We're going to the country for lunch. Dorset. It's a long drive."

"Mmm. Three hours if you're unlucky."

What, I wonder, do they talk about when they're alone? Like today, with a three-hour journey ahead of them? God, I hate the country. I always did, even as a child. And Sunday in the country is particularly abhorrent to me. A man can walk too long in the country without meeting a soul. As for animals, I'm a rural bad Samaritan. I've never seen one without wishing to pass by on the other side. Their inability to talk is particularly galling to me. Anyone who prefers animals to humans is telegraphing to the world a deeper despair than they know. No, give me a London Sunday

– one just like today when with any luck I won't see an animal at all.

"Oh, incidentally, how did it go with Alexa Richards?"

"Fine."

"Fine? Hmmm. You know she's one of Harold's old girlfriends?"

"No, I didn't."

So, that's why he pre-empted the possibility of my taking her home. Fascinating. But then men hate the surrender of power inherent in the end of a relationship. Even when they were the instigators of its demise.

"Kate, do you know the play *'Tis Pity She's a Whore*?"

"That's more Ellie's territory than mine," Kate replies.

Ellie's illness has made her suddenly feature in our conversation after a long period of awkwardness.

"Ellie wouldn't just know the play, she'd be able to quote its entire history – date of first production, who made their name in it, etc." I try to respond light-heartedly.

For a moment there is silence. Then Kate says gently, "You must miss her a lot."

"I do. I still miss her every day."

"You never talk about it. It must be harder for you than for others to talk. Difficult for you to go to a sympathetic psychiatrist."

That makes us both laugh and we're reassured by our laughter. The territory is not as dangerous as we'd feared.

"I'm sorry, Jack. It's rather late to say so but she must have found me a bit intrusive."

"Kate, I lost her. It was my own fault. I let her slip through my fingers . . . while I was thinking of other things. It's a common enough story. Women don't go back to careless men. Ian treasures her. He won her fair and square. Anyway, enough of this. The play. Do you know it?"

And I don't say what I'm thinking, that every relation-ship carries within it the seeds of its own destruction. Often it's a secret suddenly discovered, and sometimes one that's never revealed.

"Yes, I saw it once years ago. It's about a brother and sister who are in love with each other. Very violent. Horrible ending. Why?"

"Nothing. Just wanted to know. I was thinking of taking Alexa out to lunch or something. She said she's in a new production."

"Well, I *am* surprised. I thought she hadn't acted in years."

Had Alexa been Harold's messenger to me? It's a game past lovers sometimes play. Benign enough in its own way. Still, it's a further warning that he senses what others sometimes do, an exceptional, almost disturbing, closeness between Kate and me. No doubt he plays with the possibility that perhaps, at some time, there may have been more.

Everyone does. And everyone is wrong.

Nine

◆

A LONDON SUNDAY stretches peacefully ahead of me. No frustrating drive to the detested country, no small talk over lunch, no false notes to be struck by me on the beauty of the goddamn view, which demands constant comment. I am free to do whatever I please today without reference to anyone. Should I feel guilty, I wonder?

I decide to ring Rose for news of Ellie. Just as this thought pleasantly deflects incipient guilt, the doorbell rings. Cora's tense little voice informs me, with an infuriating combination of imperiousness and raging vulnerability, that she must see me. *Now*.

Cora Moore is a girl I met about six months ago, at the showing of a brutally bad film to which Kate asked me to accompany her, as Harold's flight had been delayed. His company had apparently invested money in the project. He had been assured, he told me furiously when he'd finally arrived in the appalling restaurant to which we'd all escaped, that what the British film industry most needed was a kind of updated *Get Carter*.

The film, however, was set not in the gritty north but on a vast spacecraft. The audience was subjected, for what felt like eternity, to jerky shots of the super-fit and super-stupid hero racing down labyrinthine miles of steel tunnels as he extracted revenge on a horde of lilac and green aliens for the unspeakable death of his beautiful young wife. Though they spoke no English, the translucent baddies were able to respond to "Take that, you motherfucker." Harold and an embarrassed Minister of Arts tried not to discuss the disaster and remained smilingly non-committal as the press milled around, hoping for a devastating quote for the next day's diary columns.

Cora was responsible for PR for the film. I was introduced to her, found her blonde prettiness attractive, followed the established pattern in these matters and started "seeing her" – a more ambiguous term than people realize. She would no doubt tell this story differently. Because we are caught, Cora and I, in the age-old *pas de deux* in which one person hears very different music from the other. I think she hears a kind of Celine Dion ballad, and I hear the drums. And because Cora could never break my heart, there is a distinct possibility that if I continue with this sexually satisfying on-off relationship, I might at least bruise hers.

When I come down she is standing in the hall. Her blonde hair falls straight to her shoulders. She is wearing a black sweater and grey trousers. She is very angry, and very pretty, and she is playing a game she can't possibly win. It's called "Rescue me, because I want to save you".

"I left a message on your answerphone."

"I know."

"Well, why the hell didn't you ring back?"

"I'm sorry, Cora, I've been tied up."

"That's a lie."

"Well, actually it isn't, in one sense. But in another yes, it is. It is a lie."

"How can you do this to me? I love you."

Silence.

"I love you so much, Jack. I'd do anything for you."

This is not a line I find reassuring.

"Cora . . . I don't want you to do anything for me."

No one is more cruel than an honest lover who is not in love. It's strange that through the centuries an invincible stratagem for capturing an unwilling heart has never been devised. Still, though my heart is not engaged, and I'm playing a game here, I'm still playing to win. So is Cora. We're consenting adults, and someone or other sanctioned the cruel heart if it's accompanied by the truth. Which for most of us should be refused, however hard we beg.

"Fuck you," she says.

And I half hope she'll head for the door. But she doesn't. And a million-pound industry has been built on the various ways we justify to ourselves the reason we stay – much less on the reason we're allowed to.

I put my arm around her shoulders and she gives me what is sometimes described as a heartbroken smile. I've won a mean battle. I know as Cora walks up the stairs to my bedroom that she believes I will weaken yet. And I know it's just not possible.

Ten

———

CORA LIES dreaming, a look of triumph on her face as a ray of sunshine dances down to the matted gold of her pubic hair. I wonder, gazing at that gold on gold, whether Courbet's masterpiece, *L'Origine du Monde,* would have provoked such outrage, if the exposed female genitalia had been covered by a golden fleece. Perhaps not. What's certain, however, is that for many, the concept of the Virgin Birth is psychologically less threatening and its artistic depiction infinitely more attractive.

Cora has not seduced me nor have I seduced Cora. And though neither of us has betrayed anyone, there is an element of manipulation. Each act of intercourse is another brick in the wall Cora would like to build around me. As the construction progresses, I cannot absolve myself of certain architectural responsibilities.

She believes that because she feels so much it cannot be possible that I don't feel it too. But life and art tell the same tale of the blinding certainty of lovers. The beloved *will* reciprocate and some day *will* surrender to the cyclonic power they must in time perceive to be irresistible.

I have been here before. A woman I almost loved, her name was Esther, pursued me with intent to cause grievous emotional harm, to a place I believed was secret and, with the forensic genius of obsession, found me. Furious, I took her to a hotel, ten miles away from where I'd stayed. I registered with contempt and spent the afternoon hauling her through every lust-filled dream she'd ever had of me. Until finally she said she knew it was over, that we had no chance. Sometimes only sex can make that clear. After the hours of sexual warfare which brought the relationship to an end, I drove her to the station and put her on the train.

She had the demeanour of a little girl as she sat in the carriage, looking straight ahead. For a moment I felt sorry for her. Then the feeling, like the train, slipped away. The curse of sex, its true torment, is not that it has the power to seduce us, but that it *only* has the power to seduce us. There is, alas, no pleasure or pain or mad combination of the two, which can make an unwilling man or woman stay. What is the mysterious force which makes the bond unbreakable? Perhaps it's the power of dreams. And me? I'm awake all the time.

Even with Ellie I never finally lost consciousness. My body never was more than a body, the pleasure was never more than pleasure and the pain nothing more than pain. I never dreamed of Esther. Which is why she didn't lose me. She simply never had me. And it took that strange day in the hotel to teach her that.

I know I will never dream of Cora. Because I am very selfish, I would, however, like to continue to have sex with her. What is required is a judicious redistribution of the emotional weight in order to disguise the imbalance – a Machiavellian game of sexual politics, which I sometimes play. And then I stop myself, because in the end nothing can hide the fact that Cora is going to fall.

These thoughts begin to darken this Sunday morning, which isn't going as I'd planned. Even its unexpected delights now irritate me. Cora stirs beside me, her neat little body slithering along the length of mine. This morning's pleasures will extract their price, embodying as they do irritating elements of duty.

I know a day must now be planned around Sunday morning's surprise gift. A lunch I'd wanted to enjoy alone, in my house, must now be eaten in a restaurant, or during an uncomfortably domestic hour in my kitchen. Unless I'm very careful, the afternoon will wind its undulating way to an evening at the cinema, followed by dinner and finally, probably, to bed with Cora, again.

I'd planned to ring Poppy Bright today. I wonder idly about her body – what it might look like stretched out beside me now? How shall I take thee? Let me count the ways. Is this lazily lust-filled journey of the imagination a punishment of Cora? Possibly. I take a perverse pleasure in the fact that Cora does not know my thoughts.

Cora could, of course, do precisely the same with me. She won't. The man after me, however, will be less lucky. Cora, at the moment, is concentrating all her energy on winning me. She refuses to be distracted. In Cora's case this is an act of will, far more than an act of love. She does not and cannot really love me. I cheat her of that possibility and sometimes, meanly, blame her for allowing that.

This is a shabby absolution and, irritated by how guilty she is beginning to make me feel, I decide that I will *not* have lunch with her. I will *not* see a movie with her and when she wakes up, I will *immediately* tell her the relationship is over.

Overcome with the desire to get out of bed and get away from her naked body, that seductively contentious arena, I pull my dressing-gown round me and go to my office to check my phone messages. Perhaps there is further news of Ellie.

And indeed there is. Ian's voice, full of sincerity,

expresses in that infuriating way of his, his gratitude and his assurance of Ellie's full recovery.

"We'll fly back tomorrow. All is well."

There is another message, this time from Rose, one of elegant derision mixed with an outrageous intimacy:

"Idiot man, get on with it, for Heaven's sake. Saturday proved you're perfectly adequate with children. No more than adequate, mind you. However, I now feel confident a child could survive your neurotic nature. It might even save you, my angel. You've lost Ellie, make do with second best, Jack. You've got a talent for that. 'Bye, Daddy."

I am about to switch my machine off and search for Alexa Richards's number, when another, a stranger's, voice is suddenly present in my office.

"Jack . . . Jack Trainor, is it? I've got some news for you. About Malamore. I got your phone number from your grandfather and . . . God, I hate these things. Well, if you ring me tomorrow at the office on . . . Oh, I nearly forgot, it's Shane Nolan. Do you remember me at all?"

Shock anaesthetizes. Pain comes later. There are other anaesthetics, sex, alcohol, drugs, even money. But shock has its own particular ether quotient. Reality is put in slow motion, while outlines are gravured in acid on our mind's eye.

In an effort to calm myself I walk to the window and concentrate hard on the row of perfectly symmetrical windows opposite me, each allowing a generous rectangle of light to shine on deserted rooms. So few people live here now, I tell myself. Most of the houses were long ago converted into consulting-rooms. Their occupants will arrive in the morning, followed by a continuing river of suppliants, coming to pray to the God of Limited Knowledge.

Cora drifts into the room. A bath towel is wrapped

around her naked body and she is holding two mugs of coffee. She looks fragile and pretty, like a girl in a commercial trailing an ethereal vision across the screen. The fairy princess version of the female, celestial, beckoning us to the higher region beyond earth. The one to which we will be transported if only we will buy X.

Silently, I look at Cora. I'm sure the expression on my face implies admiration, even gratitude, because she smiles at me. Her smile suffuses her pretty face with luminous certainty. Yet she is utterly wrong in everything she believes about this time and this person in her life.

Suddenly weak, I sit down. Our eyes lock, as they say, and Cora, misinterpreting my expression, places herself with elegantly sexual grace on my knee. We rock slowly back and forth. She sighs contentedly, while I try to phrase a reasonably decent sentence which will get her out of my house and my life.

"Jack? Jack?"

She is a feline creature and I'm truly going to miss her. I make a movement to try to disengage us, and her body tenses.

"Be careful, Jack. I could fall."

"Sorry."

We separate. As we both stand up, I hold my hand out to Cora to steady her. I see the expression in her eyes change to that slightly shrewd look which gives her prettiness an edge. As she bends with practised fluidity to gather the towel around her, she allows it judiciously to slip to its most becoming alignment.

I laugh. I simply can't help myself. She catches my second's vulnerability and she goes for the kill. And I think, as I lie down on her, sex will block everything out. So, just once more. Then, when she leaves I must, I really must, prepare myself for that phone call . . .

Eleven

⁓

M ONDAY MORNING. Cora leaves early to go back to her place to change for work. I promise, truly promise, to ring her tonight. We kiss. It is the after-sex kiss, which is substantially different from the more urgent pre-sex kiss, a harbinger of what is to come rather than a reminder of what has been.

Maybe I will ring her tonight. Maybe I'll ring Alexa Richards. But I know whom I must ring first. I sit quietly in my office, breathe deeply for a few minutes, then pick up the phone. "Never corner people and never allow yourself to be cornered either." My father's voice floats back from years ago. OK, let's go.

I dial the number.

"Hello."

"Can I speak to Shane Nolan?"

"Speaking."

"It's Jack Harrington."

"Ah, yes. I called you Jack Trainor yesterday. I'm sorry, I forgot."

"That's OK."

Silence for a moment. I wait for him to say something.

"I had a phone call a few months ago from a man who said he was trying to trace a house. He didn't know the name of it . . . just the general vicinity. But he did have a pretty good description of Malamore. Anyway, I told him I thought Malamore was the house he was talking about.

He asked me to let him know if it ever came up for sale. He'd be very interested, he said. He gave me the number of Savilles, the London estate agents. I was to contact a . . . here it is, top of my file . . . Guy Sanders. All this is a roundabout way of telling you, Jack, that Malamore is now for sale. Your grandfather wanted you to be told. The old get like that you know. Suddenly, everything's family. I've seen it before. Anyway he said you should have first refusal, if you know what I mean? I was instructed last Friday. Didn't waste much time, did I?"

"You certainly didn't."

"It's going to auction next month, but they might change their mind – about the auction. Only might, I'm not certain. It's a seller's market here now – the Celtic Tiger's a mighty powerful animal, Jack. Do you have any idea how much all that land your family owned would be worth now? Perhaps I better not tell you. You might never recover from the shock. Edmund shouldn't have sold off everything. Madness to sell land – that's what I say. Mind you, Jim Brosnan made the same mistake – sold off almost all the land in the early 1980s when things were tight. Malamore's nothing more than a run-down house with around seven acres of land now. Even that will cost a pretty penny."

"Why are they selling?"

"Jim died a couple of weeks ago. Left it to his niece and her husband. They live in Kerry. She doesn't want it."

"Why not?"

"First of all, she doesn't want to move to here. Dublin's in her sights I gather. They've been farming now for about ten years and she's fed up with it. She wants a different life. And people keep telling me it's available. Though I'm not so sure. Me? Same house, same town, same office and same wife. And that's how I like it. Helps me look back on a solid bank of years. I could find my way blindfold round my life and it would be a comfortable journey. I wouldn't have its edges pressing up against me all the time. I don't have to concentrate too much, I just let life run over me, like a lorry."

He's speaking in a foreign language with which I was once familiar. I'm being seduced by the rhythms and the subversive eccentricity of the phrasing, the juxtaposition of the major and the minor key, the lethal gift of the Irish when speaking the English language. One which allows them to dazzle the listener, so that you are not *quite* certain what it is that you have heard. So *caveat* listener, when a clever Irishman speaks. The women have other gifts.

I am therefore careful. I breathe slowly and say, "You're a lucky man."

"Yes, I think so. Tell me, Jack, what does Kate look like now? Someone told me once she was a model, but I never saw any photographs of her. At least if I did, I didn't know I was looking at her. Does she look like your mother?"

"She doesn't look like her."

"And you?"

"A bit like Grandfather."

"He tells me you never keep in touch. It breaks his heart."

"No it doesn't."

I want to say those lines don't work. But I stay silent.

"Sorry. Those words are stock in trade round here."

"They always were. What should I bid?"

"Will you come?"

"No."

"Telephone bid?"

"Yes."

"OK. I'll send you all the details. What's your address?"

"Send them to De Groot Collis, Mayfair." Their name comes to mind as I remember they handled Kate's South Street purchase.

"For whose attention?"

He's got me there.

"I'll get them to ring you later today."

"All right."

He doesn't say, if that's the way you want to play it, but I hear it in his voice.

"You're a psychiatrist? Your grandfather told me that."

"Yes."

"Interesting life, is it? Solving other people's problems?"

"They solve their own in the end. It's my patients who have the answer. I help them find it."

"Do you indeed? Make a lot, do you?"

I need to humour him, so I don't tell him to mind his own business.

"I do OK."

"Good. I don't suppose you've heard anything from your father?"

I hold the silence long enough to make it clear I'm not going any further with this.

"Never."

"Ah well. Can't be helped, I suppose. But I don't expect that's what you tell your patients."

"Are you looking for a free consultation?"

"Sure. If you'd like to throw it in. I occasionally worry you know, but not too much. Muddle on, I say. Muddle on. That's my philosophy."

"I like it. As a philosophy it's got a certain charm."

"Could put you out of business if it ever caught on, Jack."

I can't take much more of this banter so I stay silent. Anyway I'd better let him end it. That way he'll feel more in charge. And after all, he's done me a favour.

"Well, I'd better stop now. Oh, by the way, before I go, you can expect a letter . . . from the past. Never rains but it pours, doesn't it Jack? Phone calls, letters. Father Connolly, do you remember him? Well, he rang your grandfather, the minute he heard about Malamore − on the ecclesiastical grapevine, no doubt. And got your address from him. Power of the Church I suppose − though it's dying, of course. He wouldn't give it to me and until last week I didn't know you'd taken your uncle's name. I thought you were still Jack Trainor. Which, I suppose in a way, you still are."

I say nothing.

"Anyway," he continues, "I'll wait to hear from this . . . De Groot Collis, did you say?"

"Yes."

"OK. And Jack, you never asked me about the man, the one who rang about Malamore."

"Oh, didn't I?"

"No. Mind you, he only left me the details of his London agent. Said he wanted to surprise someone."

I bet he did, I thought. But I said nothing.

"Goodbye then, Jack. We'll talk soon."

"Thank you, Shane. I'm really grateful."

"It's a pleasure, Jack. A real pleasure."

I bet it is, Shane. I bet it is.

Twelve

—

Since Friday, events are not so much crowding in on me as raining down on me. The ground beneath my feet suddenly feels slippery. A ghostly chorus of voices, the distant clamour of uninvited guests, seems to fill the room. Hordes, I tell myself ruefully, are assembling, and with a purpose.

Grimly I search through my post, and there it is. A thick envelope, neat, spidery handwriting and an Irish stamp. I look at my watch. It's just after nine-thirty. My first patient arrives at ten-thirty. I look at the envelope again. And then carefully, with a Georgian silver letter-opener, a legacy from Edmund, I slowly cut through a thickness of ivory vellum and unfold the pages.

Dear Jack,

It was to me your father came during the forty-eight hours he was missing. There, I've said it after all these years. You, poor boy, are in receipt of that strange thing – a priest's confession.

Why now? Well I've heard the news of Jim Brosnan's death. My constant thoughts of that night and the part I played have crystallized over the years with a false, though glittering, hardness. The prospect of imminent death creates its own force-field within which much is shattered. I wish to render an account, a version of reality.

I have determined on this course of action (if writing a

letter twenty-five years after the evening to which it refers, can seriously be regarded as taking action) because with about six months to live I gather, I'm running out of time to have doubts about the wisdom of my decisions.

Old age has made me uncertain of the possibility of absolute truth. Faith yes, truth no. So here it is – a remembrance, documented with careful fidelity. In my own style I'm afraid, which meanders a little. I find that being old does not so much lead to forgetfulness, as obliterate a sense of structured time. Everything seems to run together. The way Newton's colours in soap film do, as the lightwaves from the front and back surface get in and out of phase – a memory from an old science lesson. And memory itself is like the colours, it's a dichroic mirror and creates interference filters.

I have in the past rather prided myself on the careful consideration I gave to consequences before I resolved on a course of action. Now I see my hesitancy for what it was – an escape to the life of the mind. I am that most odious thing – the pious advisor to those who live life bang up against its raw edges. A ferocious experience, from which I took flight. Celibacy was a small price to pay for freedom from that terror. The lack of responsibility to earn my living protected me from another form of insecurity. But now that the time for fear and insecurity is running low, I have only one question for myself: in all these years, did I help or hinder?

I must tell you your father wasn't looking for mercy, nor for forgiveness, and certainly not for penance, when he came to me. He did not confess to me. Though, as I have found out, confession is much rarer than you might think. An enumeration of sins is not quite the same thing. Too mathematical, if you get my meaning. But it's hard to *interfere with the style of a person's language in that dark cubicle no bigger, perhaps deliberately, than a coffin.*

And a man on his knees is not searching for further lessons in inadequacy. He is already weighted down with the ordinary sins of human life. And after confession, he will, after all, have to deal with the harsh consequences of forgiveness. Though I have found the human race in its most self-revelatory state to be more good than bad, by a significant percentage. A phrase I read the other day in Time *magazine, a subscription to which my sister's grandson in New York has kindly provided, believing that it will add greatly to my knowledge of life which he clearly regards as woefully inadequate.*

Let me tell you, that when your father stood before me that evening and told me what had happened, I silently thanked God for His gift of a vocation, which had shielded me from the possibility of such an experience. I thanked Him for the grace, which protected me from a necessity of courage, which would have found me wanting.

That evening your father, having abandoned his car in a wood about four miles from here, had walked in darkness to this village. The walk had, he said, been good for him. He said this with his old smile, as though he was referring to a morning constitutional. "I've thought it all through," he said. "I need to be able to talk to Edmund and agree everything with him. I want you to ring him, Brian. Tell him to come here so that we can talk. Edmund is the only one to whom I can entrust my children. So will you ring him now? I have very little time to save them."

I didn't hesitate. Edmund, of course, had already been informed of what had happened and was preparing to fly to Dublin. He immediately agreed to come to my house to meet secretly with your father. Though they hadn't seen each other for some time, they'd maintained contact through the years. And when your mother, his godchild (an act of reconciliation by your grandfather towards Edmund and one, alas, which he said he regretted), became engaged to your father, your parents spent a number of holidays in London with Edmund before you were born.

Your father believed that Edmund could take you and Kate away from the horror of what had happened. He believed that in that house of his in Harley Street, with its grandfather clocks ticking out the minutes and chiming out the hours, as your father described it, you two would be lulled by Edmund into a kind of forgetfulness, which he thought essential to your survival.

Your father was aware of your grandfather's unpopularity because of the Clare Loughlin affair, which many people believed contributed to your grandmother's subsequent illness and death. He thought that custody would not easily be granted to your grandfather and that Edmund would be most persuasive in the matter of your future. He also believed that Edmund could elicit from your grandfather a firm commitment to withdraw from your lives. I can't pretend to like your grandfather but in this matter he has, I believe, behaved impeccably. Your grandfather is a very strange man. When your grandmother died he asked me in that defiant way of his, "And what of the body remains, Father, after the remains have gone?" He was not the man to be entrusted with responsibility for children, and most particularly not you and Kate. As to your father's family, your paternal grandfather was already dead, do you remember him at all? And your grandmother, as you know, was an invalid.

I remember the embarrassment when reference was made to financial matters. I heard your father, suddenly hot-tempered perhaps because of his anguish, shout at Edmund, "For Christ's sake, Edmund, they're not paupers. They have an inheritance, you know." Edmund had been mortified that the subject of money should be referred to at all at such a time.

Later, Edmund left my house to go to Malamore, pretending to everyone he had just arrived from the airport. After his departure, your father collapsed in an armchair, as though the manic energy which had sustained him, had run out. I gave him a whiskey and took one myself. We sat opposite each other, either side of the fireplace like two old women, and talked the night through.

Some of the things we remembered may be new to you. I'll tell you them as well as I can. They're my memories, but you've been deprived of so much of him, they're better, I've now decided, than nothing.

I met your father at boarding school. Before we both went on to Clongowes. Did he mention St. Anthony's to you? It was set on the outskirts of a small town on the west coast, opposite a cemetery, which added a certain authenticity to our ghost stories. The maintenance of the graves of those who no longer had relatives in this world fell, by long tradition, to the juniors in St. Anthony's. The ten boys selected for this duty felt themselves honoured by the responsibility. Your father and I were two of them. The peculiar nature of this experience only dawned on me years later.

Anyway, by the time we arrived at Clongowes, your father was, as my sister used to tell me, "built". She had a crush on him and much to my humiliation she pestered him with sweets, and scarves she knitted for him in a kind of hideous, egg-yolk yellow that I can see to this day. He had enormous charm, and most people who met him were slightly singed. The priests who taught him were aware that he was, with his large, heavy handsomeness, built for pleasures they themselves had renounced – those who do not have sex do not cease to think about it. So they were erratic in their punishment and forgiveness of him. Like women.

He was funny and strong and clever enough. We formed the kind of bond that boys sometimes do. Not much said to try to plumb its depth – just a pretty good guess that he was a boy to go to the well with. Between St. Anthony's and Clongowes I spent eight years with him and we never had a fight.

And when he came to me that night it was those boyhood days I remembered and not the intermittent letters he had written to me later over the years. He presented me with the greatest moral dilemma of my life.

God, of course, always deserts us at these moments – a matter of policy, I'm sure. He probably says to Himself, have I been wasting my time all these years? Come on, man, step up to it now. It's your turn. And remember, He says to us, my own Father deserted me in extremis. Have you forgotten that I cried out to Him, Eli, Eli, lama sabachthani – Lord, Lord, why hast Thou forsaken me? So God left me alone that night and I acted as a friend and not a citizen or a priest. I did not even have the excuse that he came to me for confession. And later, I did as your father made me promise and never contacted you.

Now that time is running out for me and rather late in the day for you – I suppose you must be what, thirty-eight, forty, and Kate, thirty-two, thirty-three – here are a few of the things I learned along the way in my under-lived life. Scraps of wisdom you may still, even at your age, find useful. When I was young, I thought twenty-five was grown up. And that, by forty, one knew everything. I was wrong. It takes a long, long time to really know anything at all

about the experience. And by then it's almost too late.
Human life is very short.

Over the years I've learned that a woman can cause
havoc. A story as old as Helen of Troy or as new as
Margaret Price of Tullamore, Co. Offaly, whose exploits
with the McCaffrey Brothers were discreetly catalogued in
last week's Irish Times *and, I'm told, even in the* London
Times. *Perhaps you've read of her?*

That for some, love is an alien invasion and they feel
terror that it might sicken and die inside them.

That children disappoint as often as they dazzle.

That some people have a desire to suffer. And if they don't
find suffering in one place, they'll search for it in another.

That there seems to be more love of sex than sexual love.
At least amongst my statistically representative parishioners.
Another phrase from Time.

That you don't really know something, until you are
ready to deal with its consequences. A lesson most often
learned in your fifties, an underrated decade in which your
character finds you out.

That passionate commitment to a public cause often
provides a smoke-screen for private sins.

That unendurable illness must in the end be endured and
that what people look for when they're dying is their past.
Heaven for them is not going forward towards the light, but
backwards into the reflection of lost time and love.

That a decent lie has saved more people than we know.
And saving your life has as much moral weight as a fixation
on an impossible absolute – truth. Who can say that a life
based on illusion is any more fragile than one based on reality?

That to live your life is not so simple as to cross a field.
The line's not mine. It's Russian. I picked it up, magpie-
like, at a conference in Maynooth last year, "Catholicism in

*the New Millennium". A title I found a little confusing, on
the basis that if our ideas are not eternal, then what's the
point of them at all? Moving with the times seems a futile
endeavour when applied to religion.*

*Anyway, back to the Russians. "To live your life is not so
simple as to cross a field." Very good, I think. Very good.
Life seems to require more ducking and weaving than I had
originally believed. More strategy is required than I considered
seemly when young. I hesitate to say this, but cunning is
sometimes necessary – and I do not refer only to the political
life. Which is a life of particular fascination to men, who crave
the public acknowledgement which comes from other men.
Private applause comes from women. But the world of men
was specifically designed to take them away from women.*

*I am encroaching on your territory here. But perhaps
psychiatrists (who provide a layman's confessional, but
without that essential ingredient, penance) do for financial
reward what it is I do myself. Which is to listen, encourage,
imply forgiveness – and then get them out as quickly as
possible in time for the next visitor, whether patient or
penitent! Though, unlike the psychiatrist my penitents and
their confessor, myself, must live our daily lives in the tiny
universe of this village where I am the silent guardian of
their internal lives. Still, it works, this ability to separate the
internal and the external.*

*May I say that I feel we're ahead of the layman on the
salvation statistics. Evidently the incidence of suicide is much
lower amongst Catholics than Protestants, both of which are
lower than the statistics relating to the non-believer. A desire
to give the experience a tangible purpose is particularly hard
for those who have long despaired of God. To be fair, I have
no information as to the added benefit of the psychiatrist to
the already religious mind!*

Well, there you are, my bits and pieces from an unlived life. Throw them to the edges of your mind. They might come in handy some day.

Your father's last words to me? You'll want to analyse them I know:

"Stay away from them, as I will. No lessons from you, Brian, or long chats to seduce them back to this place. Jack will miss all the books you send him, but it can't be helped. Edmund is their guardian now. He will protect them; that emotionless, calm life he leads is what they need. Like me, they have had their fill of passion."

Those were the words. I remember them exactly.

Now I'm disobeying him. But you're formed by now and I couldn't close down shop really without telling you. Last week, Mrs. Mullally did that, closed down her little shop which sold material to the village. Gave away everything she couldn't sell. A roll of faded yellow muslin, unsuitable for net curtains, which around here must always be white, which she'd bought in an ill-judged moment, years ago. A man's tweed suit with too dandified a cut, the dandy not being an appreciated version of the species in this village. A few other odds and ends – aptly named. Then she switched off the lights, locked the door and left. She's gone. We don't know where. And those who got the odds and ends regard them now as a little legacy. Bits of nothing, really, which in a sense is what I leave you.

I'm tired now. Don't be too disappointed in me. I'll die knowing I'll be long prayed for in this parish. Your father won't be mentioned even in his own Church. There's an injustice.

My blessings to you both.

Father Brian Connolly, SJ.

Thirteen

I PUT THE letter down. Long years of dormant, almost hypnotized, inertia when even the name Malamore came to mind, resolve themselves into abrupt action, which though swift is neither hurried nor hasty. I feel myself to be an archer who has long held his bow at readiness and now releases the arrow, confident that the years of tension will increase the propellant force with which it flies towards its target. We are historical creatures and the roots of our decisions lie buried deep in our past.

Within the space of fifteen minutes I ring a shocked Shane Nolan and inform him of my intentions. He promises to act immediately on my instructions. I ring my lawyer, my accountant and my bank. I also ring De Groot's. I ring Brenda at the hospital and, to her great irritation, not to say fury, ask her to explain that I will be unable to attend tomorrow's morning session of the conference at which I was scheduled to speak. Nor will I be able to sit on the afternoon panel for questions. I quickly dictate a follow-up letter which she is to sign in my absence and hand-deliver to all the relevant people. Finally, I ring the airline and book myself on tonight's seven-thirty flight to Dublin. There is something warrior-like in all this unusual determined action. I am another version of myself and have donned rarely worn armour for a long-expected battle.

The responsibilities to my patients, which now must be

fulfilled before I leave for my own theatre of war, will be carried out with dedication, as befits a responsible man. I am my father's son.

So though today is no longer just like any other, my patients will, indeed must, break into it. I sit here in a kind of ante-chamber in which little happens, waiting for my patients to arrive with the story of great and unusual events which have taken place elsewhere. With their arrival, all my own dancing demons must be stilled. Our secret lives are most often lived beneath the lives of others. The voices of Shane Nolan and Brian Connolly must now be put on hold. My patients have to believe they sit before a man without a past. One who is dedicated to the examination of theirs. The wounded healer is not a reassuring sight.

Fourteen

—

At ten-thirty exactly the bell rings and announces the arrival of Patrick Dufors. As I greet him at the top of the stairs, his tall, edgy elegance quivers as it did last time, with neurasthenic expectation. Will today be the day on which he will make a final decision as to whether or not he expresses to his father a pent-up rage of twenty-five years' duration?

The urgency of this matter has been dramatically increased by the fact that his father is now dying, a natural enough event in the life of an adult. But this rite of passage has brought to the surface of Patrick's consciousness an ambivalent act of paternal interference, which led, he is convinced, to his deeply troubled relationship with women.

He folds himself into the chair. He speaks with the slight American overtones an MBA from Harvard bestows on second-generation graduates of *L'Ecole Polytechnique*. It is, of course, difficult for a society, which believes its language, education and culture to be supreme, to accept the fact that the future careers of their children will be vastly enhanced by a degree from one of America's leading business schools. It is a truth which sits rather uncomfortably with their constant raging against the cultural imperialism that is drowning, as they see it, the infinitely more sophisticated *vie française*. But pragmatism is a well-tested French characteristic and Patrick Dufors has until lately flourished in his banking career. Now he could destroy himself. It's an old lust, the lust for self-destruction, and the male succumbs more often than the female.

"I've just been to the hospital. It's only days now, the doctors tell me. It's going to be over soon – for him."

"Do you want that?"

"No. Not really . . . well . . . as you know, I'm ambivalent."

It's an ancient law.

"I mean, it's not that I want him to die – of course not. But he *is* dying. Soon he will be dead. It's a fact. I can do nothing about it. Look, time is running out for me as well as for him."

"Not in quite the same way."

We look at each other. There is no connection.

Minutes pass.

"You don't understand. This is my last chance. I should have tackled him years ago. Had a confrontation."

"Why didn't you? When I asked you that last time you refused to answer."

"Because . . . because he was too powerful. He seemed impervious to feelings – doubts. My mother said once he didn't suffer from depression – that he was a carrier. If I'd told him how I felt – before his illness – his contempt would have been total. I would have had to see him after-wards, with all my family around. He would have said something . . . hinted . . . mocked me . . . perhaps."

When do we ever get free of them?

"And now?"

"Now he is not powerful. And . . ."

He looks down at the carpet and I remember the saying, when the camel kneels the knives come out. Sons and fathers! First we deify the father, then we defy him, finally we deny him. Patrick now wishes to wound. Which is why he's now willing to wield the knife.

At forty, he's twice divorced. Two months ago, when his father's cancer was diagnosed as terminal, Patrick had a narrow escape from a kerb-crawling charge, which could have ruined his successful career.

He believes the reason for his behaviour lies in the fatal error of judgement his father made when Patrick was almost fourteen and on a family holiday in Cannes. His father took him to a prostitute and waited downstairs while his son was initiated into the realities of penetrative sex. At the time, Patrick's understanding of the subject was slightly less comprehensive than he had previously believed.

Though technically successful, this incident left him feeling humiliated and invaded. He felt he had been robbed of something which he could never recover. It was not innocence exactly but the dignity of his own private, first sexual experience. One which he had hoped might, in fact, occur with his cousin Beatrice – two years older than Patrick and with whom he maintains he was in love.

In fact, it has now become Patrick's obsession to find Beatrice – whom after the incident he shunned, of course. This time, he is convinced he will win her. He has already established that she too is divorced, and that she lives in Paris.

He is in agony each time he visits his father, torn between the realization that time is short, and the desire to tell his father of his rage and his hatred of him for what he did all those years ago.

So he sits there silently at his father's bedside, tempted

at the edge of eternity to demolish the reasonably civilized relationship they have enjoyed. He is certain that if he does not do so, he will never be released from the rage he still feels.

Today, while my own life cries out for exclusive attention, I listen to Patrick and wonder if it's possible to lead him towards alternative interpretations of what happened all those years ago on the *Croisette*. I need to remind him that it is the son who by being born produced the father; a white page which is written by and for the son. Do I, I wonder, have Kafka's *Letter to His Father* to give to him? After all, it was a question about sexuality which led to their estrangement. No. Best not to. Later, perhaps.

Suddenly, Patrick bangs his hand on the arm of the chair and in an anguished voice says, "God, how can you listen to this stuff day after day. Aren't you disgusted? I know I disgust myself."

"But what he did disgusted you."

"It still disgusts me."

"Yet you went to a prostitute almost immediately you heard of his illness. And you've been caught kerb-crawling. You were lucky to get off with a caution."

"I know. I know."

"Why did you go to the prostitute?"

"I think you know."

"Tell me."

"I went to remind myself of the awfulness of it."

"But you say you've never forgotten what happened. Why then the need to remind yourself? Why the need to repeat the experience?"

He says nothing. I look at his notes.

"Tell me again the date of your divorce."

Still, he says nothing.

"Were you angry about your divorce?" I ask him.

"I initiated it. Why should I be angry? I wanted to leave her. *I* left *her*."

"Why?"

"Why? Because she's a liar, that's why. I mean, Olivia was my first wife's best friend."

"But you were the one betraying your wife."

"Yes, but Olivia was just as guilty . . . I don't want to go any further with this. You're leading me away from the real issue here, which is not my divorce. Or my kerb-crawling. It's about my father. He must be made to understand what he did to me. How it twisted me. If I tell him now I will really wound him – his expectations of our . . . parting . . . will be taken from him."

"Would that make you feel better?"

"Yes. Yes, it would."

Patrick Dufors believes he hates his father, a certainty based on a false premise. Which he may or may not, in time, come to understand, so that he can forgive not only himself, but also his father, the man who may breathe his last breath on this earth watched over by an angry and ambivalent man. A man who wishes to be finished with the title, son. Too long a parenting wearies children.

His mobile phone rings. He looks at me in total panic. Then, with eyes closed, he answers:

"Yes? . . . I see. I'll be there immediately . . ."

He jumps up, puts the phone back in his pocket and, as we walk towards the door, "What should I do?" he pleads.

"You know what you should do."

"I'm on my own in this."

"So is he."

"Next week this will all be over," he says to me as he walks down the stairs.

"I don't think so."

He smiles at me suddenly, an enigmatic smile. There are moments when I am nothing more than an observer of the mystery. Which is in itself a privileged position. And no analysis of the biochemistry or anatomy of the mind or memory enables one to accurately predict the individual's unique interpretation of events.

Since he's had to leave me so quickly, I race upstairs and throw some things into a ridiculously expensive overnight bag Kate had once given me as a birthday present. Mrs. Jones is in the kitchen and I explain to her that I will be away tonight and will return tomorrow evening, probably quite late. Mrs. Jones and I get on very well. Were I to inform her I was suddenly about to take off to India for a month, she would express neither surprise nor interest. It is this indifference which I positively treasure. That I am agitated and nervous is also entirely unnoticed by her.

I am aware that this is not a condition in which to listen to Marion Masters, who will arrive in the next five minutes. I go to my consulting-room, close my eyes, breathe quietly and deeply and prepare myself for my most demanding patient.

Marion Masters's eight-year-old daughter, Amelia, was the victim of a hit-and-run driver, who is currently serving eighteen months in prison. She is writing letters of such irrepressible anguish to this young man that it is her belief that if she continues with this faithful hatred, he will kill himself. She is certain that an old wisdom is at work here, one that is infinitely superior to the conscious decision society has taken to punish the boy. Christopher is his name. Patron saint of travellers, she told me last week, and then unnerved me with her sudden laughter.

Her GP and I have discussed with her the idea of her spending some time as an in-patient. She, however, is vehemently opposed to anything other than what she describes as the concentration of her will on the breaking of the boy. Her favourite quotation, which she repeats each session, is from a ballad she was taught at school, *"Though the mills of God grind slowly, yet they grind exceeding small"*.

I shiver when I recall the session when she'd asked me if she could sing it to me, here, in my rooms. She'd promised to sing it softly and somehow the word "softly" disturbed me more than the request. I'd said yes, she could. She'd looked at me for a moment, opened her mouth but no sound came. We'd gazed at each other. It was an important moment and she began to weep. I believed it to be a turning point.

My aim, each time I see her, is gently to lead her further and further from her own arrangement of the *De profundis*. And, if possible, to achieve a slight diminution in the threnetic note of her lamentation. It is my hope that together we can slowly wind the skein back to another threshold of consciousness, from which she can, at last, begin the necessary journey to a state of mind, where what is unbearable can be borne. And where she will understand that she'll never understand.

Twelve noon. She is here. Her primitive wrath is today clothed with almost barbaric elegance, in an expensive-looking burgundy suit with a pleated skirt, which she carefully arranges as she sits in the chair. She does not cross her legs but her ankles, as though posing for a formal photograph. She is a good-looking woman, groomed to such a high level of perfection, nails, hair, make-up, that the effect is chilling rather than attractive. But then these rituals may be vital in her day-to-day battle with life, as I am aware that they are for Kate.

"I have had," she says, "a letter from the boy."

She laughs a little. The note is not exactly hysterical, but disturbing none the less. Hysteria, of course, has had a bad press in my profession, though as someone said, "It's a tough old word, hysteria, and tends to outlive its obituarists." Then she repeats the line, with the vocal emphasis on the last words, "the boy".

"Do you have it with you?"

"No."

"No?"

"No. I burned it."

"Why?"

"What did you expect me to do with it? Carry it around? Did you expect me to carry around a letter from *the boy*?"

"What did it say?"

"*It*? It said that he was sorry. He was very, very sorry. I had to laugh. I mean, I really did laugh. I must have laughed very loudly because my husband, who was downstairs, heard me. He ran up to the bedroom. My husband very rarely runs. No, I'll go further. I'd say I can't remember ever seeing him run."

"What did he do?"

"He took the letter from me."

"And read it?"

"Yes."

"You've never told him about your letters to the boy, have you?"

"No. I told you before, my husband wouldn't

understand. My husband's attitude is: this has happened; Amelia's gone; the boy lives; accept it."

"There are different ways of dealing with this kind of tragedy, Mrs. Masters. The method we decide upon is in no way indicative of the degree of grief that is being experienced."

"I regard that remark as beneath you, Dr. Harrington. I really must tell you, I am very unimpressed by what you've just said."

"You believe it to be untrue, then?"

"I do not believe that my husband grieves in the same way that I do. More than that, I do not believe that my husband grieves to the same degree that I do."

"It's not a competition, Mrs. Masters."

And suddenly I realize that for them it is. Thrown together in the drum of the turbulent threshing machine that is marriage, their different natures – she the intense and driven one; he, from her description, the more careful and repressed – have now been cruelly focused on the single, shocking event they could never have envisaged. Their marriage now is probably as close to destruction as it will ever be. And the desire of each to punish the other, for the perceived inadequacies or excesses of their individual emotional reactions, is at its zenith.

"My husband believes that since words cannot change the situation, there is nothing to say."

"Many brave men believe the same."

"You're a psychiatrist. I thought you were meant to believe in the talking cure, isn't that what it's called?"

"I do believe in it. I've spent my entire life in this endeavour. However, I am not arrogant enough to believe that this is the only way to cope. Many of those who survived appalling atrocities in war, or concentration camps, decided not to speak of their experience and to simply accept it and continue with their lives."

"My husband has not been in a war."

"It is a war of sorts."

There is a silence between us. In the past few minutes she has for the first time moved away from her obsession with the boy.

I look down at the notes.

"Who identified the body?" I ask gently, and wonder why on earth I haven't established this earlier.

There is total silence. I am tempted to repeat the question. I decide against it. The silence continues. She begins to cry. There is no hysteria.

"He did. He did."

Silence again.

"I couldn't. I just couldn't."

And I hope that it is not just because I am tired and over-wrought myself, that I sense an oscillation of hope trembling at the edges of her life, which was so brutally damaged fourteen months ago. I hang on to what I pray is not an illusion as we continue, Marion Masters and I, through to the end of today's session.

When she leaves, I feel exhausted and go to sit in the kitchen and eat the chicken sandwiches Mrs. Jones has left for me. I check my answer machine and, in an almost conspiratorial tone, Shane Nolan tells me that everything is in order, then adds, "Quick work, Jack. Quick work." And I feel like saying, no, it's not quick. It's not quick at all. It's taken nearly twenty-five years, Shane, nearly twenty-five years.

I have one more appointment this afternoon. Three o'clock. Like everyone whose work involves relationships with and responsibilities to others, my own life must be put on hold for at least another hour. After all, even the heart-broken pilot must still guide his plane safely to its destination; the jubilant nurse, newly engaged, has to minister to the dying; the anxious PA waiting for the results of her biopsy must continue to deal efficiently with the unceasing demands of her boss, as he reels his way from appointment to appointment.

We do not have the time any more to examine the great events in our lives. Which is perhaps mostly a blessing. In my professional life I have structured my own acceptable pattern of interruptions – my patients. While they remember, I forget. This symmetry, so crucial to me, is perfect. Today, however, the demands feel heavier than normal, which, of course, is no reason ever to lay them down.

This afternoon, I will listen to Oliver Banham, as I have been trained to do. As I wish to do. I will try to assemble from the lexicon of salvation, or at least endurance, words which will soothe his human hurt.

At three o'clock he walks hesitantly into the room. He is an extraordinarily handsome and athletic young man of twenty-one. The kind of young man Ellie would describe as being from Central Casting for the part of hero. And in fact, he is a hero. One who failed. For hours one night in a stormy sea, he fought to save his friend who, with two others, was lost in a boating accident. Now he battles with guilt and anger and, though this is not yet clear to him, with fear. Fear that, like Oedipus, he "would not have been saved from death, unless for some terrible woe".

Today he is shy, as young men are more often than we realize. And slowly, through the hour, it emerges that he has met a young woman at the health club he attends with obsessive dedication.

Working out, as he tells me, "To become stronger so that if . . . another occasion should arise . . . like the last one . . ."

And his voice trails off. He looks to me for some sort of guarantee that this will never happen, and we are forced back into the uncomforting realm of the "highly unlikely". The young woman is French, he tells with a proud smile. The famed allure of the foreign girlfriend is never more powerful than when foreign spells French. The notion of the *femme fatale* translates easily in most countries of the western world even if the words don't.

Unlike everyone else in his circle, Francine knows nothing of his tragedy. His dilemma is clear and complex. Silence or speech? Memory or oblivion? The decision has consequences. It could lead to a future without his old friends, or one in which Francine remains outside this circle, now bound by more than just college memories of misdemeanours, missed lectures and misalliances.

That he moves so fast after such a short acquaintance is indicative of – what? – I ask him. And he is silent. The future is not a realm he has talked about much, except in relation to the possibility that it might be waiting for him to repeat the agonies of the past. Now it has another, more positive, aura. He is drawing just a little closer to a new vision of life, and sexual desire could lead him along that way. Which is, of course, its purpose.

When he leaves, I write up my notes. I do this slowly and methodically, though I am in fact consumed by the desire to leave the house now, immediately, and start my journey. Still I delay. I return to my kitchen and concentrate on making a pot of tea, and I cut myself a slice of the ginger cake Mrs. Jones bakes each week for me.

Childish sustenance for a labyrinthine journey.

Fifteen

At six o'clock on this strange Monday, I find myself standing in Heathrow Airport at the check-in desk. By ten-thirty, having driven a hired Suzuki Vitara of an unlikely shade of green for over two hours, I find myself in a hotel I've never heard of, eight miles from the place I once called home.

The hotel was clearly designed by a dedicated follower of 1950s brutalism. One who had taken great pains to resist the undulating greensward of the surrounding hills and had placed the building in such a position that it looked strangely tilted against the landscape. Perhaps he wished to bring to God's attention the mathematical beauty of a perfect angle. It is certainly the geometric symbol to which he was most passionately addicted.

The bar is still packed when I arrive. I order a whiskey, then another. Whether through shock at what I've done so unexpectedly, or through exhaustion, I stumble a little as I pass a young woman on my way out. She turns her body towards me and I feel the sudden primitive surge of lust for a stranger.

"Sorry. Sorry," I mumble to her.

"Don't be," she says, smiling at me. "Sure, you did nothing."

I look at her and think how we've misunderstood each other. As I climb the stairs to my room, I think what a pity it is that there's no chance to rectify that. There is no possibility at all that I shall ever have her. Drunkenly I fall into bed, smiling as I listen to the echo of her words,

"Sure, you did nothing."

Sixteen

When I wake in the morning I simply can't believe
what I've done. Christ! What was I thinking of? I
pull the curtains and am lost in the landscape of my
childhood. No, I think, I'm damn well trapped in it. How
long can I take being here? For as long as it takes, as they
say. The sky, watery grey with the occasional hint of
palest blue, is as ambivalent about its intentions as I
remember. Like a mildly flirtatious woman, it sets you
wondering as to whether you're interpreting the signs
correctly.

I order breakfast and mull over the newspapers. I have
another hour to go before I meet Shane Nolan. I don't
concentrate very much on what I'm reading. My mind is
racing about wondering how I will get through the
essential visit to Malamore. I suppose I could just go ahead
without even visiting the house. But that's madness, I tell
myself. Besides, the owners may need more persuasion
not to go on to auction. How much do they know was
the question, which I'd hedged around in my terse
conversation with Shane Nolan yesterday.

"Jack," he'd said, slightly patronizingly, "it's not as if
Malamore is right in the middle of the village. And your
family didn't exactly keep open house. You were 'not of
our persuasion', if I can put it like that."

He was referring to the fact that my father's extended
family was Protestant. The persistent desire of the males

to marry Catholic women, had meant Jesuit education for the boys and convent education for the girls, in order to prove by religious subservience to Rome their passionate love of its daughters.

". . . Besides, it's twenty-five years ago, Jack. We've moved on since then. We're Europeans now. And the sad history of an old house miles outside of town has long ceased to be of interest to anyone round here, except perhaps your grandfather."

His dismissive tone was his minor revenge on me. He was entitled to it. I carefully fold the newspapers and put them back in a neat stack on the side-table.

It's time. I have no time left to pretend that the time has not come for me to drive to Malamore.

Seventeen

—

As I walk towards Shane Nolan this Tuesday morning, I am, at this moment of aberrant action, a man in total harmony with himself.

Shane Nolan has the kind of temperament that allows him to regard as completely natural the fact that I have arrived, at such short notice, in the town which I have not visited for nearly twenty-five years. Or, at least he has the grace to behave as though this is an everyday occurrence. He was, when I knew him as a schoolboy, easy-going, and seems, on the surface anyway, to have become an easy-going man. We meet as agreed at the turning to Malamore.

"You're sure about this?"

"I'm sure."

"Very well then. Let's go."

The carefree boy has grown up clever enough for his own business. He is also saying to me, you want it to be like this – that's fine by me, Jack, you cold bastard.

And I want it to be like this, because this is the only way I can do it. The harmony depends on a particular approach I know I must adopt. I must take the next few hours like a skier on a black run – disciplined but relaxed, allowing myself to surrender to the momentum of speed, without ever losing control. My mind must be like that of a Zen master, free and yet concentrated totally on the task in hand.

I will note everything, I tell myself, as a photographic journalist does in a war zone, scrupulously filming the images for later editing and transmission. There will be neither art nor artifice, no Hitchcock *trompe-l'oeil*.

As my car follows his, I do a kind of trial run for my arrival.

Now, I see myself at the open gates, then driving through them and on up the drive. I will register sycamores at the edge of the frame – quick shot of orchard garden; then the doorway, colour caught; in the hallway there will be a youngish couple. The woman will be very pretty, a detail supplied earlier by Shane. She'll speak in a rather grave manner, I imagine – for no particular reason.

I will follow them into the drawing-room – wide shot would take in most of it – perhaps someone will bring tea. After tea we'll walk through ground-floor rooms. Camera will pan up the stairs, along carpeted corridor, and briefly register each room. Finally up the short casement staircase to the master bedroom. Then I'll pan to the end of the corridor and the door to the attic. Stop.

Start again. Still filming, I'll move down to the drawing-room again. Shane Nolan will give confirmation of my intent. There will be various conversations concerning guarantees, lawyers, etc., date of hand-over. Language muffled, some technical hitch, no doubt.

Then I will leave, filming the other view – the reverse take – that of departure.

Eighteen

I STAND OUTSIDE a slate-grey house with a heavy, dull-blue door. It's a hard looking house. Perhaps only water and moonlight might detract, and then only slightly, from its adamantine power. Though the house cries out, *Stop, your journey is over*, it does not promise rest. These are the impressions of the adult and are the ambivalent gifts of maturity.

This is the place where I was born. The years of my early childhood were spent in this teeming universe of kitchen and cakes, horses and rabbits. Here lay a treasure chest of bedtime stories, the ends of which I rarely heard, drifting off to sleep, gazing at the tall-hatted horsemen and women who inhabited the wallpapered kingdom of my large bedroom. A room, which, with its stone fireplace, was identical to Kate's, in which she, too, heard similar stories.

And the gods of that universe were Catherine and Michael Trainor. My mother and father, from whom everything flowed.

My father inherited this house and nearly three hundred acres scattered throughout the county, from a childless uncle. "Take it," he'd said to my father. "It's yours – take it when I die. And don't worry about my half-sister. She made her choice when she went off to America with Dan Morrison. Anyway, I've settled money on her. I won't change my mind. I've lodged the deeds in your name at the bank. Well, who else would I give it to? Well, who? How could she be so stupid? She'd better love him. It's a long way from home if she's lost out there and dreaming of it."

I've no idea whether my father's story of how this place came to him is true. He was not, I have long realized, a man in thrall to the facts. Not through dishonesty, but because facts were rather petty matters, designed to be of interest only to those who lacked all imagination and therefore had nothing else to "fall back on". Fate had indulged him in this. He was cash-poor but land-rich – a more durable substance, he believed, than mere money. Also, my mother ensured that a life of petty facts and dutiful farming was kept at bay by her passionate intensity, which nurtured the essential dreaminess of his nature. How could reality compete?

Today, a silence, not necessarily sinister, lies like a vast stage curtain across the front of the house. The air is permeated with the nervous expectation of a first night audience, which I'd often witnessed with Ellie, as the chatter dies seconds before curtain-up on a new play.

Shane Nolan and I move awkwardly round the uneven courtyard, each of us waiting for a denouement. Glancing purposefully at his watch and in a determinedly confident tone he assures me, "They should be here any minute. I've got all the papers."

He pats his briefcase. He is armed for the fray.

"They wanted to meet you here. They felt it was more appropriate. God knows why. Do you want to go in while we're waiting?"

"No."

I walk away from him. He feels too close.

"Thanks," I say, looking back. An insultingly obvious afterthought, which I regret.

"You're welcome."

I don't blame him for the note of exasperation in his voice. I am a difficult client, unyielding and uncommunicative. I walk over to the side of the house, where a redundant paddock fence marks out an area now devoid of horses.

"They're here," he calls to me, unnecessarily.

"Yes," I reply. It's a superfluous affirmative. I'm not the only one who is nervous.

The car sweeps into the courtyard, a little too fast. They are eager to sell, I tell myself. I walk towards Shane Nolan and take up a slightly proprietorial stance in front of the house, which once, in childhood, was mine, then Jim Brosnan's and is now theirs. The house which will, I hope, be mine again in a few hours.

Mrs. Daly virtually bounces out of the car. Shane Nolan is right. She is a pretty woman, with creamy skin and blonde curls tumbling almost into her eyes. It's the hair-style of a child, but it's a wilful, knowing little face that smiles up at me. I smile back and it is clear from her expression that the heiress – as I would guess she now sees herself – wants the money. That predatory little face is alive with the joy of impending wealth. Unlike my father, she intends rejecting the bricks and mortar of her inheritance. For a price. I search her expression further for a sign that she understands what a wise decision she has made.

"Well, you've given us a great surprise, Mr. Harrington."

"Actually, Ita," Shane says, "it's Dr. Harrington."

"You didn't tell me that, Shane! Sorry, Dr. Harrington."

Tell her to call you Jack, I say to myself. Yet, even as she invites me to call her Ita, I decide against this step towards familiarity and informality. I'm convinced I need to keep her slightly supplicant in this situation, in which, in fact, she holds all the cards, or in this case the deeds. After all, until I have them in my hand, anything can happen. I try to take the sting out of what she may interpret as unfriendliness by commenting profusely on the prettiness of her name. She seems perfectly happy and, with an air of fluttering busyness, comes straight to the point.

"Did Shane tell you that we were going to auction until we heard of your generous offer?"

"He did. I'm pleased you find the offer acceptable."

I sound slightly abrupt I know but I need to do this quickly.

"Oh, we do, we do. I suppose we could play games and try to get more. But we're not like that, are we, Brendan? We're not greedy people."

She shakes the curls for emphasis. Brendan, clearly bewitched by their white-gold undulations above the ice-blue eyes, confirms this character assessment.

"Not at all. A fair price, that's all we're interested in."

Considering I have offered substantially above what Shane Nolan had advised me was the maximum price an auction was likely to produce, it's an enchanting charade and one I would have enjoyed more under different circumstances.

"Shouldn't we all go inside, Dr. Harrington? You've got the keys, Shane?"

"I have, Ita."

We start moving towards the front door. Can I bear to walk in with these people? Is there anyone with whom I could bear to walk into this house? No. Get away from me, I want to shout at them. For a second I almost panic. Then I realize what I must do.

"While we've been waiting, I've looked over the house. I hope you'll forgive me, Ita – Brendan . . ."

I look at each of them with only a slight air of apology. Any more would unbalance the power play in this fledgling, though vital, relationship.

A confused Shane Nolan is about to contradict me, sees my face, and stops. I continue, speaking very quickly.

"I have no doubts at all. It's exactly what I want. Shane has all the papers at his office."

Again, Shane moves to contradict me and is just about to pat his bulky briefcase when I say, "If you'd like to go there you can look through them. I gather you've already talked to your solicitor. I just want to have a walk around the gardens. In case I want to go into the house again, would it be all right for me to have the keys? I'd be so grateful,"

I look from one to the other, with what I hope is not a pleading smile. Ita smiles back at me – a trifle flirtatiously.

"Of course you can," she says. "To tell you the truth, I'm pleased not to have to go in myself at the moment. I only visited once or twice as a child and I found the house quite scary. I'm amazed Uncle Jim left it to me. But I suppose he never married and he had no children. He was always kind to me when I was little and he came down a few times to see us in Kerry. I'm quite sad about him really."

Though I'm quite certain she'll get over her grief, I try to sound sympathetic.

"I understand," I say.

Why did he leave her all this, I wonder? The yellow curls, maybe. That ancient coinage.

I have no idea whether Shane Nolan is angry with me or not, because I determinedly refuse to meet his eyes. And I've no idea if, finally, it's the businessman protecting the deal or the old schoolfriend who decides to play along. But play along he does and does it very well.

Their cars turn away from the house and within minutes the sound of tyres on gravel is lost. In silence, I walk slowly to the front door, turn the key in the lock and step inside.

Nineteen

L ONG AGO and here, in the house where I was born . . .
here in this vast, cold hall . . .

. . . my mother, swaying slightly, walks down the wide
iron-balustraded staircase, moves across the hall towards
my father and, almost in a whisper, she says:

"Michael."

He does not turn round but stands quite still by the
window, looking out at an expanse of green with a dark
sky, like a grey shawl, floating above it.

"Michael?"

Still he does not move.

She walks slowly towards him until she is standing
directly behind him. Suddenly, and without turning
round, his arms stretch out behind him and he grasps her
round the waist. She flattens herself against his back and
they rock wordlessly forwards and backwards. He releases
her and turns to face her. Then he spreads his hands out
and places them on her breasts. Smiling at her, he slowly
guides her backwards to the wall. She falls against it and
he kneels before her and raises her skirt.

"Well now, Catherine Trainor, did anyone ever tell
you that there are many forms of worship?"

And he buries his face between her legs.

Then he stands up and, quickly unbuttoned, spread-
eagles her against the wall. They move together in a silent
and desperate gyration, that seems at one moment to beat

her rhythmically against the wall and at another to raise her, pierced, legs dangling, not noticing as her shoes slip off and fall, as they themselves finally do, exhausted, on to the stone floor.

After some time she slips from under him and skips to the stairs, swishing her skirts extravagantly, like a Spanish dancer. She stops almost at the top and pirouettes round to face him, laughing. The sound is like Kate's wild laughter when she's jumped a dangerous fence.

"Catherine! Be careful! You could fall."

"Never, never while you look at me like that."

And his laughter seems to run a race with hers up and down the staircase, as though caught in a mad, dangerous game. They seem to laugh their way across the landing and I hear their footsteps on the short casement staircase to their room, and finally, the sound of their bedroom door slam shut.

Suddenly, a side-door is flung open by Tom the farmhand, who lives in the gate cottage. Kate, wearing jodhpurs, her hair tamed into a single plait down her back, runs in after him. As she stands on tiptoe to put her jacket on the hall-stand, the plait looks like a red wound on her mud-splattered white shirt.

"Your father's going to rip into that brother of yours when he finds out he didn't come today. I've other things to do on my Saturdays, you know. I'll get it in the neck as well for not finding him and hauling him out, and just throwing him on the damned animal. This is the fourth or fifth time he's done this. Where's he hiding anyway? You can tell me now, Kate. It's too late to take him out."

"Oh no, Tom. We never tell our secrets. We're blood brothers."

"You're a girl, Kate. You can't be a blood brother."

"Yes I can! Jack says it doesn't matter. Jack says as long as you mix the blood and never let each other down it makes no difference you're a girl."

"Jack says, Jack says . . ."

My father descends the stairs and strides into the hall. He pulls her pigtail playfully. When I do that she kicks me on the shins.

"Well, Kate, you'll find out some day there's more to life than what Jack says. There's what your father says for a start. And what your father says is, you go and find that blood brother of yours and tell him it's time for lunch."

"Don't be cross with him, Daddy. He just hates riding."

"I'm very, very cross with him. His mother will be furious as well. You tell him that. And tell him I'm going to give him a terrible beating. Thanks, Tom. I'll see to it he'll be there next time. Be patient with him. 'Bye now. And, Tom, I know it's not easy."

I crawl from my hidey-hole, a vast dark wooden cupboard with broken-slatted back and doors. It was manoeuvred on to the landing once to hide a crumbling patch of damp, which now bears the imprint of my bony elbows. Through the chinks in the almost-black wood, I have witnessed something I do not fully understand and do not want to understand. Shaking a little, I slip along the narrow back corridor to my bedroom where Kate finds me. Full of fear and worship, she tells me I must come down to see Daddy, who is in "a fit of rage with me".

Whistling softly, eyes down, I walk towards him. When I look up at him, he is my father again and not the man I saw earlier.

My mother seems to fly down the stairs, agile and angry

145

as she hears the story of my missed riding lesson. She too is my mother again, the one who flies in and out of happy/angry like a bird leaping from branch to branch. Everything about her is so fast and up and down that we are never quite certain how she really feels. Except we know that only he can tame her. And that we have no power over her at all.

"Tell me where you were, Jack. Tell me this instant!" She's like an angry bird now.

"It's a secret."

"Kate? I insist you tell me."

"I can't, Mama. I've sworn an oath. I'm a blood brother now."

"Oh, for God's sake, Kate." My mother looks as though she might stamp her foot, a sign of real trouble to come. Kate looks to my father for guidance. He always knows what's the best thing to do. He's never wrong. Kate knows that. So do I.

Then, turning towards my father, my mother says, in a fierce voice, "Make him tell us, Michael."

"Very well, Catherine. Follow me, Jack."

My father takes the leather belt he always uses for this purpose and closes the corridor door firmly in the faces of my stern looking mother and of Kate, who runs to a corner and hides her head in her hands.

I follow him down the short, back corridor that leads to a lavatory "for visitors", though we don't have many. This narrow, dark place has long ago been designated the special spot for the purpose of punishment.

"All right, Jack," my father says, in a loud and frightening voice.

"Now, don't be too hard on him, Michael," my mother calls from the hall. Her mood has changed in seconds – as it often does. Now she sounds close to tears and I can hear Kate crying:

"Oh, Daddy. Daddy, please don't hurt him."

My father raises the strap high above him and brings it down hard against the wall. I jump, as I always do, at the sound it makes.

"All right, Jack," he whispers. "You do your bit now."

I howl like an animal as my father beats the wall three times. At the third beat of leather on stone, I run to the bathroom and splash my face with very hot water, as he taught me to do years ago. When it looks red enough I stop. I don't touch it with a towel, just shake my head, like a dog, to dry myself. Drops of water, like tears, remain.

He lifts my chin when I come out, examines my face carefully and tells me to pinch my cheeks a bit. Then we saunter towards the door. He whistles softly. I try to copy him but now fail. Though when I'm alone, I can do it quite well. Still, I'm happy. I'm very happy. He is my real blood brother as well as my father. And this is our big secret.

"Every household needs at least the pretence of the stern father. My great and clever friend, Father Brian Connolly, told me that when you were born. He's a member of the Society of Jesus – an elite corps, Jack. They study for fourteen years before they're ordained – and it's generally believed that on subjects theological they're the tops. Of course, study was no great problem for Brian, who preferred reading to life. Don't make the same mistake, Jack, with all those books Brian keeps sending you. Anyway, I think his advice was based on his years of study of the Ultimate Stern Father – you know – the one who sent His Son down to die for our sins. A bit tough – wouldn't you say? – a bit tough. Now listen, indulge me in this will you, Jack, go with Tom for those riding lessons. And Jack, you can keep your secret. A man's entitled to a bit of privacy, eh?" He winks at me.

We're in the hall again and I run to my mother, as he told me to do, from the very first time years ago we played our secret game. She pets me. I wriggle away; I feel that she does not want me too long pressed up close against her.

"Well, Catherine, I think you'll find Jack won't miss another lesson. Will you, Jack?"

"No, Daddy."

"Good. Now let's all go into the dining-room and have some lunch."

We sit down around a huge, oval mahogany table in the dining-room. My mother and father sit side by side at the curved top, closest to the door. I sit on my mother's right and Kate on his left so that we face each other, but must turn our heads a little to look at them.

Sarah has brought in the dark-red leather box, in which what he called "demands" are kept, and hands it to my father.

"Oh damn! Is it that time again, Sarah?"

"It is indeed, Mr. Trainor."

Sarah, the housekeeper, came to Malamore with my mother. She once told me my mother was worth "ten of him". For years, I thought she was talking about money. But then, as my father often says to me when she's harsh with me, "Sarah doesn't think much of men, except Tom, of course." She's always in what we now call "a bit of a haze" so there's never any point in asking "Where's Sarah?" She's in bed, resting, which now she does nearly every day, particularly in the afternoon. "She's in love with the bottle, I'm afraid. It's true love – let's hope it's not for life."

Today, she looks grim.

"Thank you, Sarah. I chose the box myself, for this very purpose. Note the colour, children. It's a fighting red, my darlings, a fighting red."

"Right. You asked for it," Sarah says grimly as she places it in front of him. "Ring the bell when you're finished and I'll bring the lunch."

"OK, Sarah. Right, children, let's look at these demands. Let's see if Armageddon is just around the corner, shall we?"

"What's Armageddon, Daddy?"

"Well, Kate, it's what people wish on those who are having a better time than they are. And who, therefore, should be punished."

He takes each piece of paper, holding it up with both hands as though it might fly away, then places it face down between the box and his table-setting.

"Part of Aunt Beattie's little legacy this time, I think. Yes, we'll hire those acres out. That should do the trick."

"Oh, Michael!"

"Yes, my love?"

"Be serious."

"I'm serious only about you. Only about you," he says, blowing her a kiss.

"What about us?" Kate can't bear to be left out.

"Oh, I'm never serious about you two. You're funny little things. You're not serious at all."

"He's joking, darlings. He's very serious about you both." Sometimes, only sometimes, it's Mother who says the things we want to hear.

But my father's had enough of the red box, and rings

149

for Sarah, who comes in looking "hazy". Today he doesn't seem to notice, though yesterday I heard him say, "She's got bottles hidden all over the place."

"Thank you, Sarah." He hands the box to her. "I'll do the cheques in the morning. Well, children, that's so you know not to be afraid of that red box. And, my darling Catherine, let me tell you that we're not doing badly, not badly at all. You tell your father that, will you my angel? Look smug if you can – for me."

"What's smug, Daddy?"

"Smug is a very, very vulgar little smirk, which you should only indulge in when you simply can't resist it."

"Oh Michael!"

Their laughter seems to explode around the table. Kate and I join in.

I am ten and a half and she is nearly five and life is perfect.

A rainy Easter Monday, teatime, and we are thrown around the sitting-room eating tea and cakes.

"Is that the telephone, Daddy?"

"It is, Kate. You've got great little ears, haven't you?"

He strides out of the room into the hall. And we giggle as we listen to him go through his ritual. Even my mother smiles with us. It's a secret smile – almost like a blood brother would give.

"Johnny. Is it tomorrow you're coming? Great. Don't worry. Have you got a piece of paper? All right, then. You know how to get to the town . . . well, by that stage, you're nearly with us. We're almost exactly four miles outside town. So, set your mileometer when you drive over the green bridge. You'll pass the hospital a mile after that. Then two miles on you'll come to the graveyard.

Didn't they plan it well, the town planners? First the hospital, then the graveyard. Then you'll come to St. Columba's, that's where Jack goes to school. Kate's at the convent; the other side of town. Another perfect bit of planning, if the Bishop had any say in it, which I suppose he did. Anyway, where was I? Or, more precisely, where were you?"

He laughs, happy with his little joke. Kate and I start to laugh as well and our mother puts her finger to her lips to silence us.

"Had we got you past the graveyard? Ha, ha, ha. Ah, yes. St. Columba's. Take the first right down the lane. It's marked but you can barely see the sign so don't bother looking. Well now, at the end of the lane you'll come to iron gates. Press the bell at the side and Tom will let you in. Or, if he's in the fields, his wife Sarah will open the gates. Then drive very slowly up the avenue. I'm ordered by Catherine to tell you that, because Kate and Jack might be roaming around by the time you get here. If that makes them sound like wild animals, you've got the picture."

He laughs again and calls out as he crosses the hall and returns to the sitting-room, "That was Johnny. He's coming tomorrow afternoon. But this afternoon I've got the pleasure of your grandfather, children. He wants to talk to me privately. You two go off out and play. Catherine, why don't you go up now, angel, and have a little rest."

And Kate, her red plait flying, runs after me and we play hopscotch in the yard. All the time we listen out for the scrunch of our grandfather's car on the gravel. There it is! Kate and I look at each other and, giggling, climb in a side-window. Trembling with excitement we hide behind the heavy hall curtain and hold our breaths, hoping to hear another battle between these two giants.

Our father's shoulders are almost as wide as the door. We know that his big smiley face, which glows like Santa Claus's on Christmas cards, will not be at its happiest as he opens it to my grandfather, an even taller man. A man who, we have long ago decided, could not be more different from our father. A man my father once said who should never have been a doctor, since he believed the time spent on his patients could be better spent on himself.

Grandfather is the thinnest man we have ever seen. He always wears long coats, even in summer. Perhaps to cover how thin he is. The collar of his coat seems to hold his head at some strange, proud angle as though he was looking down on everything and everyone. The only soft thing about him is the spill of white hair, like milk across his forehead. Perhaps it's all that whiteness that makes him seem a winter man.

As they walk across the hall, Kate and I hug each other at the thrill of what is to come.

"I've heard some rumours. And I'm worried. I know my daughter."

"So do I." My father's voice is angry and sarcastic.

"She is . . . craven . . . in these matters."

"Jesus! How can you talk like that about her?"

"Because I know her better than you do."

"Like hell you do!"

"I'm not here to cause trouble between you two. I never wanted you for her, but that's over now."

"Is it? I don't think it's ever over."

"Well, I've accepted you."

"You had no choice." We can hear my father pacing the hall now.

"I knew that! Even when she was only seventeen and being chased by far better men, I had to watch her throw herself from one corner of this county to another after you. So, I'm telling you, I'm ordering you, even after all this time you've been together – be careful with her."

"This is man-to-man advice from you?"

"No. Father to husband."

"Indeed. And, as always, with her best interests at heart."

"Yes. Just like you. And you could do her a great deal of harm."

"As she could me. And you were hardly the perfect father."

"I know the pain I caused her."

"No, you don't."

"Well, that's past. There's nothing I can do about it now."

"Obviously. Clare Loughlin is in a mental institution. And Catherine's mother is dead," says my father. His footsteps have halted.

"That is so."

"That is so! Where the hell did you learn to speak like that? How did you learn to be so cold?"

"Medicine. It makes you cold. Too many defeats."

"You hypocrite! Your great defeat has nothing to do with medicine. You have a dead wife and an institutionalized mistress. Hell of a legacy for a country doctor."

"My patients forgave me."

"Not all of them."

". . . No," he says quietly.

"But they had nowhere to go. Dr. Rogers wasn't here then. You were in an invincible situation. But when Rogers came it all changed, didn't it, Frank? All those husbands who wondered what it was you took into the sick room with you."

"You know, Michael, that's the meanest thing I've ever heard you say in your life. You know perfectly well the only woman I ever loved was Clare Loughlin, and that was well after she'd ceased to be a patient."

"I'm sorry. You bring out the worst in me, Frank. I'm sorry."

"Shall we stop this now? I've heard the rumours about you and Phyllis Mangan. And if Catherine hears them as well . . ." They are moving towards the sitting-room.

"For Christ's sake, Phyllis Mangan is my mother's nurse! I see her when I visit. And yes, she flirts with me." My father's voice is louder and angrier.

"That's not what she told me."

"What are you trying to do? Are you trying to cause friction between Catherine and me? Are you trying to tar me with the same brush as yourself?"

"Phyllis Mangan is no Clare Loughlin!" Grandfather says this very slowly and though he's not shouting he sounds just as angry as Daddy.

"This is insanity. You destroyed your wife's life because of a woman and managed to destroy your mistress as well. And because you've always hated me . . ."

There is a sudden silence. Then, the noise of a chair scraping along the stone floor and my grandfather, speaking very quietly, says, "A woman? Is that all Clare Loughlin seemed to you? A woman! She didn't seem 'just a woman' to me. She was one of the three Loughlins. They were like the Three Graces. Do you remember their names from that expensive Jesuit education your Catholic mother forced on you against your father's wishes? And which you seem to have put to no good use."

My father remains silent.

My grandfather speaks again.

"Aglaia, the shining one; Euphrosyne, the cheerful one; and Thalia, the blooming one. Clare was Aglaia to me, the shining one. And my God, she dazzled me. I had a passion for her, the way men do. What is it in us that make us feel we cannot live if we don't have them? I've examined the human body from its pre-natal stage right up to the moment after death, and I haven't found a trace of the disease. For disease it is. It's incurable. And because of it, when I'm dying, I'll remember her, only her."

"Well, that'll be a great bloody comfort to her."

"You listen to me just this once, you spoiled land-owning bastard. You did nothing to deserve your good fortune. You were left damn near three hundred acres and you've even added to it over the years – charming those decaying bachelor-uncles of yours, falling in on themselves with the effort of deciding who should inherit their land. And what do you do with it? You're hardly bothered to visit the smallholdings and check what the hell is happening. You trust everyone because you're too goddamn lazy not to. You hate farming so you just half play at it. When you get into debt, you sell or rent. You overindulge your two children . . ."

". . . And I make your daughter very, very happy."

"I made her mother happy – in the beginning. That's why I'm here. I'm here to do you a favour. As well as Catherine. She saw it all when she was young. What she saw and heard may have left her vulnerable to a kind of fear that it might happen to her. That she too might be abandoned. You were her great ambition. She was ambitious to live the greatest love story in the world, with all the ferocity at her disposal, which as you know is

155

considerable. It's a dangerous ambition for anyone – never mind someone like her."

". . . Married to someone like me?"

"Women come to you. I've had to fight for mine."

"They may come to me, Frank, and I've had my temptations, but Catherine is my whole life. Her and my two overindulged children. Today, I'm going to give you the benefit of the doubt and take it that you are really trying to be helpful. Look! The rain's stopped now. Come for a bit of a walk with us. After that Catherine should be awake and we'll have a drink."

They start to walk back towards the front door. When we hear the door bang shut we clamber out, hearts pounding and almost collapse on to the concrete below. And as they turn the corner of the house we giggle hysterically, partly through the excitement and partly through terror at what we have just heard. My father stops and looks back at us.

"Listen to them! They go mad when they play hopscotch. Come on, you two, we're going for a bit of a walk with Granddad."

We follow obediently.

After about half a mile my grandfather, suddenly looking at his watch, swears, "Christ! Is that the time? I've got to be off. You carry on. Goodbye, Michael. It was a strange conversation, but I'm glad we had it . . . well, goodbye, you two."

"'Bye, Granddad."

And we are alone with our father and trot along beside him, Kate swinging from the hand of this mysterious man whom "women come to". This marvellous man, who is our father. And we forget about our "craven mother", though we have no idea what craven means.

As we turn into the narrow lane, which leads to the high oak door to the kitchen garden, we come face to face with McGreavey's huge alsatian. Paralysed with fear, we remember that Sorcha Caffrey, a girl at Kate's school, had been savaged last year. McGreavey's the local police sergeant, so nothing was done about the dog. Now we've cornered it. "Never corner an alsatian – they revert to their nature, which is that of the wolf," our father'd told us over and over again. The wolf-dog's head, with its high-set ears, seems to narrow from his angry eyes to his nose and jaws as though all the power in him is concentrated there. He isn't growling so we cannot see his teeth but we know from the stitches in Sorcha's leg what he could do to us. I feel I'm going to be sick and Kate starts to whimper.

"Stand still, you two. Don't move! *Don't move!*"

He's whispering, but it terrifies us more than if he'd shouted.

"We won't, Daddy."

"Don't shout! Speak softly, if you have to. Otherwise, say nothing."

"Yes, Daddy," we whisper.

"Now, I want you to take a small step backwards. Let go of my hand, Kate. Shush. Now, slowly, one step."

Almost on tiptoe we step silently back.

"Good," he whispers. "Another one."

We barely breathe.

"Yes, Daddy."

"Kate . . . don't cry, Kate."

"No, Daddy."

"Back a bit more now . . . slowly . . .

". . . *Kate!* Don't cry, not so loudly, Kate." Suddenly and without any warning, she bolts, the way Ashes her favourite horse did once. And though he whispers it, his voice is so full of fear that he may as well have shouted, "DON'T RUN, KATE. DON'T RUN! Oh Jesus . . ."

McGreavey's alsatian starts to growl. It's a horrible sound. Then it makes a sudden leap and we see its black-and-brown-coloured body swinging and twisting wildly from Daddy's arm, which he's raised up across his face to protect it.

"Daddy! Daddy!" we scream.

"It's all right, children!" He tries to say this quietly but it's like he's gasping out the words. "You can run now, quickly. Get Tom. Tell him to bring the gun."

"Yes, Daddy."

And as we run for Tom, we hear him cry out, "Get down. Get off me." And we hear sounds, which we run away from, faster and faster.

And then, more faintly:

"Children . . . Kate, Jack . . . Don't tell your mother."

And even fainter:

"Oh, Christ . . ."

"Tom! Tom!" we scream. "Daddy's in the lane. McGreavey's alsatian's got him. He's bleeding, Tom. Get the gun, Tom. Daddy says get the gun."

Tom looks at us, stunned for a second, then runs to his cottage and races down the lane with his gun.

"Hold on, Michael. Hold on," he calls.

Though Tom shouts at us not to, we run after him but can't catch him.

Then from round a bend in the lane, a shot. Tom comes into sight, supporting Daddy, whose arm is a ragged mess of clothes and blood, which drips in an almost perfect line of tiny red splashes to the ground, like coloured rain. When he sees us, he cries out, "Ah, children. You shouldn't be here."

And as we approach the house, "Mrs. Trainor, ring for your father," Tom calls.

"Don't sound so panicky, Tom, sure it's nothing. Don't frighten her."

"Like hell it's nothing, Michael."

She stands transfixed in the doorway. We run to her, of course, calling, "Mama, Mama."

She puts her hands out as though to ward something off – something she doesn't want to know.

Grandfather returns and gives our father an injection. And carefully binds his arm up, so that he looks like a wounded soldier. We sit, elated, Kate and I, in the kitchen looking at him, the romantic, bandaged hero. Our father is a hero and he is now safe at home. And when Grandfather leaves to deal with another emergency, it all seems perfect. We will all have supper together. Maybe in the kitchen, which will be lovely. Suddenly, my mother, who'd sat silently through it all as though she were in a kind of trance, breaks in, "Michael, why didn't you move back slowly? I don't understand it. Why didn't you just move back slowly?"

"I was trying to, when that bloody animal leapt."

"Liar!"

"Catherine! Stop now, Catherine."

Then, looking at us, "Go on to the sitting-room, you two, we'll be there in a minute."

"You're very brave, Daddy."

"Well now, Kate, you're pretty brave yourself."

"No I'm not, I ran."

"You ran? *You ran?*"

My mother is almost screaming at Kate, who looks frightened, as though she's about to cry.

"I didn't run fast, Mama – I promise."

"Don't you know anything? No one runs when they corner an alsatian. You stupid, stupid girl. He could have been killed."

"Stop it, Catherine!"

"What would I do without you?"

"Oh, for God's sake, Catherine! Children, go to the sitting-room, go on, now . . ."

And as we scurry down the hallway:

". . . Oh, Michael, I was terrified – when I saw you bleeding and . . . Oh, I'm so sorry. I'm so sorry."

"Shush, shush, angel. Darling, darling Catherine. You've had a terrible shock."

Mystified, Kate and I look at each other. Daddy'd had the shock. Wasn't that right? Wasn't that right? What is it that we do not understand?

I am nearly twelve. She is six and a half. What is it that we do not understand?

"DADDY, DADDY!"

It's the middle of the night. I run down the corridor to their bedroom. I switch on the light.

He is lying on top of her, naked. The blankets and the top sheet are thrown on the floor. There is a slow separation and an animal-roll to the other side of her. For a second I see her damp and glistening and stretched out lazily.

He does not leap up, embarrassed, to cover himself. He slowly gets out of bed and walks to where the sheet lies on the floor, picks it up and wraps it round him and throws the blanket gently over her.

"What is it, Jack? Is something wrong?"

She says nothing. She just lies back on the bed, her eyes on the ceiling, listening as though someone is telling her a story.

"I had a terrible nightmare. I'm sorry. I'm sorry."

"Don't be sorry, Jack. I had nightmares till I was sixteen. It's a sign of a good imagination."

"I'm OK now. I want to go to the bathroom. Will you see me down the corridor?"

"Sure, Jack."

He follows me down the corridor. I open the bathroom door.

"I'll wait outside for you."

As we walk back to my bedroom, there's a question I have to ask him.

"Daddy," I whisper, "when will the hair come?"

"Oh, a year or so, maybe two. Are you dreaming of the hair, Jack? You shouldn't worry. You're between childhood and young manhood, and that's a strange, dreaming time." And then he laughs.

"But I should warn you that when the hair does come, oh, you're in trouble then, Jack, I can tell you."

"Trouble? Why?"

"Why? Women, that's why."

"But why?"

"Because . . . oh well, we'll talk about it soon."

Women? I think, women? Is Kate waiting for hair too?

There is a sudden clap of thunder, followed by rain rattling on the window.

"Look at this downpour, just at the wrong time. Farming makes you a victim of God at his most capricious. His moods, dark or sunny, can ruin your year. I prefer to surrender to the moods of your mother. A man's got to make a choice, God or a woman. For those of limited vision, I suppose it must be God."

He pulls the curtain back across.

"Oh heresy, heresy. Anyway, you'll have to make your own mind up later on."

"After the hair?"

"Oh, years and years after the hair."

"How many years?"

"So many years you'll have forgotten about this conversation."

"And women? Who do they choose? Do they choose God, or a man?"

"Well, they tell you they choose God, but don't believe them."

"What kind of men do they choose – when they choose men?"

"Well, some of them choose a man with land, or a business or a profession."

"Did Grandma choose Grandpa because he was a doctor?"

"I think so."

"What happened to her?"

"The doctor made her sick. Ha, ha, ha."

Then, looking down at me, laughing:

"Sorry, Jack, forget I said that."

"And Mama?"

"Mama – well, she's a woman. She's what a woman can be . . . she . . . she's my God."

"Will I get a woman like her?"

"Do you want a woman like her?"

And a vomit of guilt runs over me when I say,

"Yes. Oh yes."

And mean no.

I am twelve and a half.

"I think we should be more careful. They're older now."

They're in the kitchen. I've run back, slipped away from Tom who'd taken us out on a rabbit shoot. I'm trying to sneak into the house to my hidey-hole. I crouch outside the back door and push a bit against it, so that it opens just an inch or so. The heavy, dark green draught-curtain barely flutters as they talk in that strange voice, which is different from all their other voices, whether cross or happy.

"They're on the rabbit shoot. And Sarah's in one of her hazes. Anyway, what are you saying to your darling, that she is reckless? Am I a reckless woman, Michael?"

She is giggling now.

"Did poor Michael Trainor marry a reckless woman?"

He starts laughing with her.

"Poor Michael Trainor just doesn't know what to do with his reckless wife. Let's see. Come here to me . . ."

"Here? Here and now?"

"Yes, here," she says.

"But the children," he mocks her.

"I told you they're in the lower fields on the rabbit hunt."

"I wonder if they'll ever know which one of those fields is our field?"

"No. They will never, ever know." She sounds as if she's dreaming.

"Shush, shush. Come here, Catherine."

Silence.

"Am I hurting you?"

"No. No."

"Is the wall cold?"

"It's icy. I'm freezing and now I'm burning."

"Don't move, Catherine. Stay still. Stay totally still. I just want to whisper things in your ear – turn your face slightly to the door, no, not your body."

"Lean on me more, press me into the wall. I won't break, Michael. Oh God, my stomach is freezing."

"Don't move."

"You're heavy on my back."

"Good."

"It's like a song – I love, love the word heavy." She sighs as she says this.

"Did you hear what I've whispered?"

"Yes."

"Listen again."

Silence.

"Life is only this, isn't that true?" she asks.

"Yes."

"For you as well as for me?"

"For me as well as for you," he tells her.

"Can I move?"

"Yes."

"Now?"

Sounds.

"Are we perfect?" she asks.

"We're perfect."

"Purely perfect?"

"Oh yes."

Silence. How long? I don't know. I'm almost too terrified to breathe.

Then his voice, "Want a glass of water, goddess?"

He must be at the sink, just above where the kitchen window looks over the paddock. Because suddenly, and in a voice which now sounds normal:

"Here comes the golden pigtail! All legs and arms and that flying plait. And wait for it . . ."

I scramble round the side of the house as Kate kicks the kitchen door open. I hear her shout:

"Daddy, Daddy. I shot three rabbits. I shot three . . ."

I sneak past the kitchen door, jump the small stream and then, creeping behind a hedge so they can't see me, finally get to the paddock. I climb the fence. Then I stand up and brazenly run down the path. Dramatically out of breath, I slam the front door and burst angrily into the kitchen.

"Tom didn't wait for me . . ."

"What do you mean, Tom didn't wait for you . . ?"

Now Tom has joined us.

"Listen here, Jack," Tom says furiously, "don't you try that on with me. It doesn't work with me. You tried to give me your gun and said you wouldn't shoot any more rabbits. That you were going home."

"No, I didn't."

"OK then. Where's the gun?"

"Where's the gun, Jack?" My father sounds angry.

I say nothing.

"Jack! This is serious. I want you to tell me now where the gun is."

I know from his face it's serious. I trust him. So I tell him.

"It's round the corner of the house. Leaning up against the shed."

"Thank you, Jack. You'll never do that again, will you? Leave a gun lying around?"

"No, never."

"Michael, he really must be punished for this. To make him really understand."

My father looks at her and for once shakes his head.

"No, Catherine. Not this time. I know Jack. I see in his face that he knows the seriousness. He'll never do it again."

And then he smiles at her.

"It's a man-to-man thing, Catherine. It's a kind of code of honour, isn't it, Jack?"

"It is, Daddy."

"You'll find out more about that when you go off to Clongowes in September. You'll have to make a lot of important decisions about people, who to trust, who not to trust, and I won't be there to advise you."

"But I'll write to you all the time, Daddy."

"I know you will, Jack. I know you will . . . Now Jack, back to today. Are you trying to get out of rabbit shoots now, Jack? You used to love shooting."

"Not any more. Anyway, Kate's better than me . . ."

"Ah, so that's it, male pride. Well, I suffer from that a bit myself. Fatal business, male pride. What do you think, Tom?"

Tom, glowering at me, says, "Male pride, my——"
He's about to swear. Thinks better of it.

My father, to the rescue again, "So Kate's a great shot then?"

"Well, she could be. She's brilliant one minute and useless the next," Tom tells him.

"She's a bit erratic? Well, it's a woman's privilege."

"Did you do what Tom told you?" My mother sounds anxious as she turns to Kate.

"Yes, Mama."

"You must always obey Tom. He knows all about guns. He's there to teach you. So you listen to him. It's dangerous otherwise."

"Yes, Mama."

"Promise me, Kate."

"I promise." Kate turns away, rolling her eyes so that Mama cannot see.

"I'm off now." I can see from Tom's face that he's had enough of this scene.

"Thanks, Tom."

"That's OK."

"Say thank you to Tom, children," my father says.

"Thank you, Tom," we say in unison.

"Can we do it again tomorrow?"

"No, Kate."

"Why not?"

"No need," my father tells her.

And my parents look at one another. I think I understand.

I'm thirteen.

Kate and I are squashed against the wall of my hidey-hole behind the cupboard. I promised I'd let her join me if she too would trick Tom and run away.

"Michael! Michael Trainor. You answer me. You answer me now."

My mother's voice! They're coming up the stairs. Now they're just down from us on the landing.

She's angry. Her hands, small fists of rage, are beating him.

"Jesus Christ, Catherine. What the hell are you doing?"

"I'll beat you all around your heart. I'll bruise and break it into pieces."

"Don't, Catherine. Stop it."

"Stop it? I want you to stop her."

"Who?" he asks.

"Phyllis."

"Oh, Phyllis."

"I want you to stop her."

"Stop her what?"

"Stop her following you. For the past three years that woman's been following you around – looking at you. Stop her looking at you like . . ."

"Like what?" We can hear the smile in his voice.

"Like she wants you."

"She does want me."

"How do you know? Did she come out and tell you at last?"

"I know the same way you know – her eyes, the look in her eyes."

"Well then, don't look into them."

"What do you suggest I do? Keep my eyes on the floor every time I see her?"

"Yes."

"Jesus, Catherine. I have to see her when I go to my mother's – she's my mother's nurse. She's very kind to her."

"Fire her," my mother says angrily.

"No."

"Fire her."

"No. Come here to me."

She moves towards him.

"I can't help it," she says quietly.

"I know."

"I just can't help it. It's how I am."

"No, Catherine, darling Catherine, it's how *we* are."

"Oh, Michael, you're a lovely man. So, Michael Trainor, let's dance."

"Here, on the landing?"

"Well, we're only seconds from the bedroom if anyone comes to the door."

And she takes her clothes off and folds them and puts them neatly on the landing chair. He does the same. In the silence, their bodies move towards each other. Something seems out of balance. Maybe because, as I've just learned at school, converging lines produce distortion. His back is to us. His shoulders hide her face. They dance towards the other side of the landing and turn. Now he is facing us. Suddenly he stops and she is on her knees before him, as though she is worshipping him. It is a mystery. Mysteries must be respected. I know that. Kate hides her face in my back. I gasp with fear as my eyes absorb a vision of pain. His face is horribly contorted, almost knotted in what seems to be agony and he pulls her hair tight from her head as though he's falling and she's his lifeline.

I close my eyes against it. I stuff my hand in my mouth to stop my sobs. Kate digs her head deeper into my back.

When we open our eyes again, they're gone.

I am fourteen. And she is eight and a half. It is a Thursday in August.

Sunday, August 14th, 4 p.m.
I sit rigid on a high-backed chair. An hour ago it was carefully placed, by my father, exactly opposite Kate's in the stone hallway. We do not speak or even whisper to each other. Silently, looking only at each other, we go over and over the words we know we will eventually utter. In the meantime, we sit and wait.

As my father told me would happen, Tom has given up beating on the window. He couldn't open any door or window because my father has locked them all. I know, since he also told me, that Tom would go for help. It won't take long. We wait.

We hear the sound of cars. Now we hear men's voices and the beating on the door gets louder and Tom is calling to us again.

"Jack! Kate! Open the door. Come on, now. Come on now, children. Open the door."

Still we do not move. Now we can see Tom with two policemen standing behind him, banging on the window. Suddenly, a policeman breaks the glass with his truncheon and turns the handle of the window. Tom climbs through, runs to the front door and releases the bolts. The policemen enter.

And I know that our house is their house now.

I see blood drip to the floor from the cuts on Tom's hand. He comes towards us but stops. Perhaps there is something in our faces. He walks towards the staircase followed by one of the policemen. We hear them walk across the landing towards the small casement staircase that leads to our parents' bedroom. Then we hear nothing.

Perhaps they've gone to the attic.

The other policeman sits in the middle of the hall, like a prisoner. His head is bowed and his hands are locked as though he's praying. He remains, like us, still and silent.

Later – is it after only minutes, or much longer? – Tom and the policeman come down and Tom shows him where the telephone is kept. And we hear them talk to Dr. Rogers. I am surprised they do not ring for my grandfather.

Then we hear another car. The sergeant runs to the window. I hear him swear.

"Christ, Harrington's here. Oh, Jesus Christ."

He runs to bolt the door again. Kate and I look at each other and we almost smile as we hear our grandfather banging on the door. Now he's at the broken window. They won't let him in. He screams at them.

"I know something terrible's happened. Jane Dunne

saw your cars racing here. Let me in. They're my grandchildren. Where is she? Where's my daughter?"

"I'm sorry, Harrington."

"Oh God. Let me in. She's my daughter, for God's sake, man. She's my daughter."

"I'm sorry, Harrington. You'll thank me later."

"It's that bad, is it?"

The sergeant says nothing.

The sound of another car.

"That'll be Rogers," the sergeant says.

"Rogers?"

"Yes, Harrington."

"It's that bad, is it?" he asks again.

"Listen, Harrington, let Rogers do this. If you let him pass, you can come in and sit with the children. That's a promise."

"And Catherine?"

"You can see her the second Rogers is finished. Is it a deal?"

"It's a deal."

He looks smaller now, my grandfather, as he follows Dr. Rogers into the hall and stops beside our chairs. Dr. Rogers does not talk to us but walks on and up the staircase accompanied by the sergeant.

Our grandfather moves between us, forwards and backwards.

"Kate? What happened, Kate?"

She says nothing.

"Jack. You tell me. What happened?"

I say nothing.

We neither of us look at him.

Suddenly, Dr. Rogers is at the top of the stairs and calls down:

"Tell Dr. Harrington he can come up now."

"I'm grateful, Rogers. I won't forget what you've done here today."

He sounds humble. He's never sounded humble before. And we listen to his slow footsteps on the stairs, as though he is climbing a mountain, step by step.

The sergeant tries to move our chairs closer together. We don't want that and he stops. He motions to the young policeman to get up. Then he sits between us.

Looking at Kate, he says, "Kate, would you like some water?"

"Yes, please," she says politely.

"John, get the wee girl some water."

The young policeman follows Tom, who shows him where the kitchen is.

"There you are, Kate. Have your fill of that. And Jack, would you like some water?"

"Thank you."

John, again accompanied by Tom, who doesn't seem to know what to do or say, returns to the kitchen.

"There we are, Jack. Did you notice he brought a larger glass for you? That's because you're a man."

"He's a boy. Daddy's a man."

"And where's Daddy now, Kate?"

Silence.

"Jack, where's your father now? Did he say where he was going?"

Silence.

"How long ago did he leave?"

We say nothing.

"Well now, Jack, they tell me you're great at school."

"Who?"

"Who, what?"

"Who told you?"

"Bridie told me."

"Where's Bridie now?" I ask him.

"At home. Let's forget about Bridie. You tell me what you did since you came back from church. Slowly, in your own time."

"Do you want a glass of water as well, Sergeant?"

"Be quiet, John, will you! I don't want water. I just want to hear what these two children have to say. Jack, Kate; slowly in your own time."

"I don't want to talk. I don't want to talk." Kate is crying.

"It's all right, lass. That's all right. Jack, what about you?"

"When we'd had lunch, Mama went upstairs to rest."

"Does she always do that, after lunch?"

"No, just on Sundays. We're allowed to watch television if it's raining. And then Daddy went upstairs as well."

"And then what happened?"

"We heard shouting. It got very loud. We went upstairs. They weren't in their bedroom. We went up to the attic. We're not supposed to do that. The shouting had stopped. They were dancing."

"They were dancing? Are you sure?"

They look at each other. We nod.

"Was there music?"

"They don't need music."

Silence.

"And then what?"

"They stopped dancing. Mama got very cross again. She was hitting Daddy."

"Maybe she was only play-acting. Just pretending. What do you think, Kate?"

Kate, suddenly gushing words, "No, no, no. Mama was hitting him. She was hitting him – round his heart, she said. I was frightened. I wanted to stop her. I hid behind Daddy, after Mama fell over. After . . . after the . . . sound."

"Sound of what?"

"The gun. The sound of the gun."

"Who had the gun?"

Kate looks puzzled for a minute.

"Daddy, of course."

"And what happened then?"

"Daddy scooped me up, like he always does when I fall – it's our special scoop. Then he brought me into my room and I took off my cardigan and dress so that he could rub ointment on my shoulder and bandage my arm. I got all bruised when I fell over. Then he helped me wash my face and knees. He said I couldn't put my dress back on again 'cos it was dirty. It's my best dress, which I only wear on Sundays.

"I told him I didn't mind but that Mama would be very cross when she got better. But he scooped me up again and gave me a big hug and said he was certain Mama wouldn't be cross but that he didn't think she would ever get better. I asked if that meant Mama was dead and he said yes it did and that he had to go away to make 'rangements for us.

"Then he took Jack into his bedroom and talked to him. Daddy promised it would only take a minute. So I waited outside. Then we went downstairs, all together into the hall.

"Daddy got the chairs and he gave me a big kiss and put me on this chair and told Jack to take that one. He told Jack not to take his eyes off me. He told me not to think of anything except that I was the best and prettiest girl in the world and that Mama would be looking down on me forever. And that wherever he was he would be thinking of me day and night. Then you came . . ."

"Is that right, Jack? What Kate's said?"

"Yes."

"How long ago did your Daddy leave?"

"I don't know. I couldn't see the clock."

"And do you not have a watch, either of you?"

"Daddy took them. He said it would remind him of us wherever he went."

"And he took the gun with him, did he?"

"Yes."

"Have you got all that, John?"

I look over. The policeman has been writing in a notebook.

"I think I've got it, sir. It was a bit difficult what with the wee girl speaking so quickly. But yes, I've got most of it."

My grandfather and Dr. Rogers are now back in the hall.

"I think we should get them out of here now. Tom, where on earth is Sarah?"

"She's at her mother's."

"Ah."

Turning to the sergeant, my grandfather says, "I'd like to stay here with her. I'm in no fit state to drive them to my house. Can you do that? Maggie, my housekeeper, is there. I'll be along later."

"I'll make all the arrangements," Dr. Rogers says. "Dr. Harrington can stay here with me and I'll drive him home later."

"Thank you, Rogers."

The sound of more cars arriving. The young policeman now at the window tells the sergeant, "It's Father Keane *and* Canon Brown."

"Both of them? Indeed!" For a second, my grandfather's voice sounds the way it used to before . . . before now.

"Kate, Jack, you come with me. I'm going to drive you to your grandfather's. Maggie'll look after you until he arrives."

And since I have no more instructions from my father, I take Kate's hand and we follow the policeman out of the door. Still holding hands, we sit quietly in the back of the car. We do not look back as we speed away from the house. We know that we will never, ever go there again. We know that our life there is over.

I look at the clock in the policeman's car. Quarter-past six. The rain has stopped. It's now a bright and sunny Sunday evening. Some people walking along the road peer into the policeman's car as we pass and I know for sure, looking at their faces, everything's different now.

When we arrive at our grandfather's, even Maggie is different, kinder, fussing over us in a way she never did before. And late at night, when we're in bed but not asleep, a man we're later told to call Uncle Edmund arrives. He is our grandfather's much younger half-brother, whom we've only met once before when we were so young we barely remember. And there is a row, which we cannot bear to listen to.

The next morning, there are phone calls, which we do not understand. There are more visits from policemen. They go over what we told them yesterday. Then Uncle Edmund won't let them ask us any more questions.

And then we are in Uncle Edmund's car. Our

grandfather does not stand at the door to wave us off. Though he watches through the window as the car turns out of the gate. We cannot tell whether he is crying or not. But he looks sad.

We are very quiet during the drive. Uncle Edmund does not ask us any questions at all. We are at the airport. We're in an aeroplane, which we've never been in before. Then a taxi. And at six o'clock on Monday evening we walk up the stairs of a tall, narrow house in London. I ask Uncle Edmund where we are.

"You're home now, with me. You're in London. In Harley Street."

It sounds nice.

Twenty

"WHERE TO?"
          "Harley Street."

"It's going to take over an hour . . . traffic's hell this morning."

I glance at my watch. Nine-thirty. My first appointment is at eleven. I can just about make it.

I didn't fly home last night as I'd intended. I got waylaid by the girl in the bar. I was drunk. Drunk with exhaustion; drunk with elation; and most of all, drunk with memory. And memory is at its most overwhelming when we surrender to it in the very place which once trapped raw experience. As I had done yesterday, in Malamore. The only thing I wasn't drunk with was alcohol.

After I'd left Malamore I'd driven – too fast – to Shane Nolan's office, where I'd signed some preliminary papers under the attentive gaze of Ita's cousin, a solicitor who'd driven down from Dublin, "especially for the purpose". I'd staggered back to the hotel, having "shaken hands" with Mr. Daly and his now rich-and-thrilled, flirtatious little wife. Her excitable eyes had been glued to the fax machine, as various papers whirred through from London. Papers, which she'd signed with a magnificent flourish and a triumphant smile to her husband. The balance of power in that relationship had most emphatically changed. I'd wondered how Mr. Daly was going to handle the suddenly altered dynamics of his marriage.

The young woman who'd assured me that I'd "done nothing" the night before was in the hotel bar, drinking coffee, when I'd returned from my strange, sad victory. I'd ordered tea and sandwiches and sat on the banquette close to her.

"You look happy and lonely at the same time. How do you manage that?" she'd asked.

"Years of practice."

"It's a good trick."

"I think so."

"Where do you come from?"

That question rather caught me off guard. Normally, of course, I'd have answered London. However, I'd hesitated, wondering if I dared say to her that actually "I come from round here".

"Here and there," I'd said. An accurate description.

"Most people do."

This quickfire repartee had reminded me of Ellie. Women like this excite me. They are the very antithesis of Kate. And the excitement they engender in me has nothing of the terror that accompanied my mother's thrilling presence.

"I'm Jack," I'd introduced myself. It was the kind of minimal introduction this particular encounter required.

"And I'm Deirdre."

"Of the Sorrows?"

"Know your Irish literature then?"

"It floats back. Sometimes."

"And will you float back?"

"No," I'd said.

"Fair enough. A girl likes to know where she stands."

"Where do you think you stand?"

"Oh, probably on the edge of making a fool of myself. But it's a position I'm familiar with, so don't worry. I keep my balance in the end."

And I'd remembered reading somewhere that Freud believed psychoanalysis to be wholly wasted on the Irish, because they understood themselves so well already. After all, it was hardly a country calling out for the talking cure.

"That's reassuring," I'd said. Then added, "I'm going back to London first thing in the morning. I won't be back. I don't think this conversation would work so well in London."

"You're right. But it passes the time now. And my mother used to say, now is all we have. Shall I give you my vital statistics?" She was laughing as she'd said this.

Her laughter was infectious.

"Sure."

"Well," she'd said. "Thirty-four – years of age. Divorced, civil action, available now of course. One son, a perfect ten. Boarding-school. Nothing but the best for Rory, his father's name. I still like it. Is this an outline that delights you?"

"I find it totally seductive," I'd replied.

And with the introduction of the word "seductive", the game was over. Both of us had won. And in the new Ireland it was possible for us discreetly to spend the night together. And we did.

Twenty-one

⌒

"HOW MUCH?"
          "Thirty pounds."
I hand over fifty pounds and say, "Take thirty-five."
I unlock my front door and greedily inhale the particular aroma of Harley Street. It's a combination of decades of wood-wax and silver and brass polish. Pelargoniums add a distinctive bitter-sweetness. Edmund used to call them geraniums but the florist's daughter, who has a degree in horticulture and now runs the business, does not respond to a request for geraniums. And I've long ago given up the battle. Anyway, it's a heady brew, a kind of incense, and slows me down.

I need to be slowed down. For the past thirty-six hours I've been spinning purposefully towards a shrouded destination. And during that time my breathing and my heartbeat have slightly changed. I must get back to my old rhythms and disciplines. The ones which save me.

I'd resisted breakfast on the plane so I make myself a quick cup of coffee while Mrs. Jones prepares toast and honey for me. Nursery food, again.

The bell rings and I become my best version of myself; the self which listens, observes and searches in the cadences of an hour-long conversation with a patient, the potential outline of their salvation.

So today, Wednesday, this strange Wednesday for me, eleven a.m., welcome back Sir George Bywater. Behind whose eyes reels of the movie, which once starred his now dead wife, Alice, play to an empty cinema. One to which time has brought a competing attraction, the voluptuous Patricia. She is now the living, breathing, walking, talking woman of the moment. Sadly, even Alice's silent era may be drawing to a close.

He starts. "This is difficult. In fact, I really don't know how to tell you. I can't imagine what you'll think of me. I . . ."

He throws his arms slightly up in the air. It's a marvellous gesture, which implies, "It's out of my hands now". Though, as yet uncertain what "it" is, I know from his expression that he's happy. I wonder did his grief and anger fall accidentally, or did he just throw them away? Either way, Sir George Bywater is a very different man from the one who visited me last week.

I smile slightly at him. He needs no further encouragement.

"It's Binkie!"

"Binkie?"

"Alice's sister. I told you about her. Lives in South Africa."

"Yes, I remember. Murder capital of the world."

"Yes, well, she's back! She's in London. It's astonishing. She rang me on Saturday – day after I saw you, remember?"

"Yes, I remember."

"We met up for dinner, Saturday evening. Mark's Club. Marvellous food. Have you been there?"

"No."

"How can I put this . . . ? The marriage is over."

". . . The marriage?"

"Yes. Her marriage. Her marriage is over." He sounds triumphant.

"He's been having an affair for ages, evidently. God, what an idiot! I mean, what an idiot to lose Binkie! She's fantastic. Did I tell you that the last time? She's absolutely fantastic."

I say nothing.

"She said she wants to stay with me for a while. Until she finds her feet, you understand. And it simply flooded over me – things I'd long forgotten. How I'd always adored her, her laughter, her wildness, her . . ."

". . . Similarity to yet subtle . . . differences from Alice?"

"Christ, how did you know? I said some indiscreet things to her. She didn't stop me. In fact, she said, it's always been there, hasn't it, George? And of course, it's true. Always, underneath my life with Alice . . ."

". . . Always?"

"Well, maybe I exaggerate. But you know, just something . . . kind of unresolved."

And I think how we rush towards the light – however illusory. It's healthy. It's ruthless. It's an imperative. Though it's not for everyone.

"I'm certain, absolutely certain. Binkie's for me! I know it will work."

He looks at me. He wants affirmation. I remain silent. He frowns. He's irritated. He does not want any criticism, either spoken or unspoken, of his new arrangements – his bridge to a new life. I glance at his notes. Binkie – her father's favourite? Yes, there it is. Poor Lord . . . ? I realize I don't know his name, this father whose second daughter is about to become involved with a man of whom he most certainly does not approve. Daughters! Dangerous creatures. Particularly for fathers. They introduce a different tribe into the mix, one that may take over. It's a primitive reaction, of course, but the resentment lingers still.

"And, of course, the children! They adore her. Absolutely adore her. Which is a huge, huge comfort. You see, it's not a chopped-up life any more." He sighs, almost delirious with relief.

"Binkie was marvellous, absolutely marvellous, at the funeral. Did I mention that?"

"No, you didn't."

This was not the moment to remind him that he'd spent most of the last session discussing his difficulties with Trisha. Or Pa-tricia. The change of nomenclature, which had been the single triumph of his otherwise ghastly weekend of almost a fortnight ago.

He continues excitedly with an exposition of Binkie's remarkable qualities, as though he were carrying out an actuarial assessment.

"It's not just that she's incredibly attractive and sophisticated. It's that she's so goddamn nice! I mean, she told the children wonderful stories about Alice. About the Alice they didn't know. Teenage Alice, that kind of thing. She made them laugh, actually. She's astonishing. Everyone says that about Binkie."

"Forgive me . . . Are you still in a relationship with Patricia?"

I need to come straight to the point here. George Bywater is almost hysterical in the contemplation of this new, marvellous life that has suddenly descended upon him in a period of two or three days.

"No. I'm not."

"I see."

"I took her out to lunch yesterday and I told her that I just didn't think it was going to work out."

He's a man of action. Particularly when it comes to his self-interest. He is divesting himself of unprofitable company in order to marshal his resources for the more fruitful expansion of his empire. Synergy. He's looking for synergy.

"What reason did you give?"

He looks away from me. After a short silence, he says, "The children."

It's a tough old world.

He talks on for the rest of his allotted hour about the way his life now feels "connected". His old life with Alice will flow more naturally into his new life with Binkie. The children will be content. And he's probably right. They've won a victory. They've extracted their price: Patricia. I wonder if she'll go back to being Trisha? That symbolic surrender hadn't worked. And that time in Menton when she'd interrupted the conversation, disturbed the dynamics of the long-established friendships, whose tentacles had spread deep into their professional lives as well – that had been the shape of things to come. An unappealing outline to Sir George. Poor Trisha. Clever, but not quite clever enough.

Finally he leaves, bounding down the stairs. He wishes to see me two weeks from today. He's right. This drama is far from over. And its resolution will take a long time.

As soon as Sir George has left, I dial Harold Abst's business number. I'm put through immediately, which I would guess doesn't happen to everyone.

"Harold, I'd like to see you. Urgently, if that's possible."

He doesn't ask why.

"I'm tied up all day and have a business dinner this evening. I'll be home by eleven. Can you meet me then at Eaton Square?"

He has the grace to imply that he's asking me if it's a convenient time. I like him more and more. As I put the phone down, Mrs. Jones, after a peremptory knock on the door, enters with an enormous arrangement of white orchids. They spring to attention from a moss-topped metal container. The sudden geisha-like blossom is in strange contrast to the seemingly desiccated stalk.

"Well, well," she says. "This is quite a display."

Mrs. Jones, though impressed, does not actually approve of display. She stands there hoping that I will read the card and say, "Oh, they're from . . ."

I know who they're from, Mrs. Jones. She is reluctantly sensitive to the nuances of my silence and she leaves the room.

The card reads:

> *You were, as always, kind and generous.*
> *Love and gratitude,*
> *Ellie.*

I dial her number.

"Jack! You were so wonderful to take the children. I can't tell you how grateful I am."

She sounds really well. I feel relieved and refreshed and suddenly confident enough to tease her gently. The way I used to when we were happy. As indeed we were. The miraculous intimacy we shared did not have the time to generate into resentful emotional bondage.

"Say that in French."

She laughs.

"I'll say it in every language I know. *Tu es merveilleux, Du bist erstaunlich, Eres maravilloso, Tu sei magnifico* - am I making myself clear? You are, and always were, marvellous."

There is a moment's silence. I hesitate on the brink of saying something . . . inappropriate. She catches the beat and rushes in . . .

. . . She is glad to be home and will cut out any overseas trips until the children are older. She appreciates Ian's commitment to the family, his passion for the children. She's happy to fit her own ambitions around the life they've created. She really enjoys radio work.

I let her continue with this hymn of praise to domestic life and its joys and sacrifices. I do not say that a short trip to three major European cities can hardly be regarded as an act of daring irresponsibility, though God knows I'm tempted. Ian really is a pain in the neck, selfish, jealous of every minute she's away. I restrict myself to, "Ian will be pleased."

There is a short silence. Then, my clever Ellie says, "It's my ideal life, Jack, selected from others which were, and indeed are, available to me. I know the other routes. They don't lead where I want to go."

What does she mean "were available to me"? I used to be so jealous. I'd watch her talking in German or Italian to some entranced guy at a dinner party. He'd probably felt restricted by his stilted English, not realizing that stilted English, and as little of it as possible, made one the ideal guest at most of them. Anyway, Ian can live the jealous life now. Good luck to him. God, I'm a sour loser.

"Mother tells me Kate is getting married." Ellie says this carefully.

"It looks that way. To Harold Abst. Rose said she knew his father and keeps in touch with his uncle."

"Well, that's one way of putting it."

"How do you mean?"

"Well, let me put it the way Mother does. When she

was young, she had a very close relationship with Bruno Abst. They worked the territory together. That's an exact translation. Or would you like it in the original French?"

"What territory?"

"Post-war Europe, Jack. A veritable patchwork of opportunities and pitfalls. They were comrades in arms, no pun intended. After Mother came to England, he went to the Middle East; as they say in the story-books, both of them lived happily ever after. Though not with each other."

"Why did I never meet him? Why didn't you mention him? Come to think of it, I don't *ever* remember you mentioning him."

"Well, he's rarely in England and anyway, Mother told me they'd vowed to keep out of each other's family life. Unless there was a crisis and they needed each other. So I've only met him once or twice, in between divorces, etc., on their way to little lunches, *à deux*, always *à deux*, darling. You know Mother."

"Not as well as I thought."

"Do you think this will work out for Kate? I always felt wary of her, but I suppose you knew that?"

"Yes. So did she."

"I know. But you were so very close to her. It made me uneasy. Anyway, we had other problems. Perhaps we should have seen a psychiatrist?" she says teasingly.

"Very funny! You rather pre-empted discussion."

"Mmm. Yes, it's my technique. I think secretly for a long time. Then I act. It's a bit cruel, I suppose. Still, about Kate; let's hope it works."

". . . And I mean that *most sincerely*." I mock her again, as I used to when we were happy.

She laughs. "OK. OK, but when she's finally settled, so

to speak, you should think of getting married again. It's a pity Esther didn't work out."

"Wow. Good comeback. You haven't lost your touch, Ellie. Quite the little killer when you want to be."

"I'll go further. You should have lived with her, persuaded her to stay with you in Harley Street. She might have succeeded where I failed."

"Ellie! That was almost Rose-speak!"

"I try to resist, most of the time, but now and again those genes just come burstin' through. Before this gets completely out of hand, I'm going to thank you again for being a knight in shining armour and surrender to an afternoon of recuperative rest watching Fassbinder's *Effi Briest*."

"Is your German still up to the original?"

"It was when I read the novel. I think I've won this little skirmish, Jack."

"I'll give it to you – 'cos you're sick."

"Ouch. And goodbye."

She matched me. And she still does. And that idiotic banter kept me on the surface. Which is the safest place to be sometimes. And then I lost her. And that's that. There were others, of course, Esther being the most important. But I ended that one afternoon in a shabby hotel, surprised to find in myself such depths of cruelty.

Anyway, it doesn't matter which way I tell it to myself, Ellie left and no one else has taken her place. And when Ellie left me she was pregnant with Margaret, though I did not know it at the time. Whatever a woman tells you at the beginning, and believe me, they will tell you anything at the beginning, when it comes to children they are more determined, more focused, more subtle and infinitely more strategic than any general marshalling his troops for the final assault. And why not? They have their eye on posterity from their earliest days and are well-practised in tactics by the time they're ten.

Mrs. Jones enters the room with a chicken salad and a bottle of San Pellegrino. She glances surreptitiously at the orchids as she places the tray in front of me. Clearly she regards me as a most unlikely recipient of romantic gestures. I feel mean not to tell her who they're from but I don't want to start a conversation about Ellie. Mrs. Jones leaves the room in a slight huff.

As I eat my lunch, I rock forwards and backwards in my chair trying to compose an ideal opening to the vital conversation I will have later with Harold Abst. And, apart from the words, I ponder my tone. What exactly should my tone be? How should I sound? Should I sound sad? Burdened? Wise? Friendly? But not so friendly that he believes I will forever be the third walking beside them.

This will be a crucial conversation. I've put so much into this endeavour, not only over the last twenty-four hours, but also for the last twenty-five years. I don't want to blow it now.

I could begin "Harold, I really should have told you this before. I feel very badly . . ." No, that sounds too pleading. "Harold, for the first time I feel confident of Kate's future. It's been a big responsibility – a joy, of course." No, that's all a bit coy. On and on I go, turning over beginnings in my mind, hoping I will remain in control long enough to achieve the desired end.

The bell rings. It's two-thirty. Janice Dwyer is here. I'm on duty again. Harold, Kate, my plans and stratagems, must now be put aside. I must be totally available to Janice. She deserves nothing less.

Janice Dwyer may very well be in the early stages of anorexia nervosa. Marion Masters would, I know, have little sympathy with her illness. Marion Masters is consumed by the purity of her agony and Janice Dwyer, were she to listen to her, might hang her head in shame or terror. But Janice may lose her life if she moves any closer to the edge of a compulsion which devours the starving and is never satisfied.

She wears a red sleeveless dress with a loose chain belt around her hips. The dress is heavy and tailored and since it does not cling to her body, it is her arms, today surprisingly bare, hanging like white piping on either side of the dress, which tell her story. Her legs are cleverly covered in soft leather boots which come almost to her knees.

Her voice is surprisingly strong, mature even. Sometimes in our sessions it is only the strength of that voice which gives me hope. I have to be more careful with Janice than probably any of my other patients at the moment. Janice is here at her mother's insistence and not at her own request. Getting her to agree to another session is often the trickiest part of the hour.

Today, things seem to go reasonably well. In fact, I feel quite satisfied as I walk her to the front door, having agreed on the same time next week. As I am about to close the door, she suddenly turns on the steps and says, with what seems like an innocent smile, "Everyone keeps telling me to get a life. But you know what I say – whose life should I get? I don't see a fucking life around me that I'd particularly like to take."

I'm pole-axed for a second.

"Your own could be a good place to start, Janice."

What the hell have I just said? Did she get the *double*

entendre? Her expression doesn't change, so I continue, "Want to talk about it a bit more now?"

"Poor you. There's not a thing you can do to make me come back up. And there's not a thing my mother can do. I'm an adult and I'm only border-line, you know. Don't worry, I'll be here next week. We can go through a list of lives. What do you think? Think we'll find one?"

And she runs down the street, laughing.

At three o'clock I ring Shane Nolan as promised.

"Shane, things were so rushed yesterday I didn't get a chance to thank you properly. You've been terrific."

"Well, I'm pleased you're pleased." He's wary still. My sudden friendliness is a little too late for him. He can sense the falseness. He knows he's there to be of use. I decide it's best to come straight to the point.

"Shane, when everything's finalized, would you be interested in supervising the demolition and then recon-struction of Malamore? I want to convert it into apartments. It's clear the town has grown. We could get four, maybe six . . ."

". . . Christ! You never said a thing about that. You never mentioned a word about gutting it. How on earth can you even think of gutting Malamore?"

"I'm sorry. I thought I had mentioned it. It was a hefty sum, Shane, and it's meant to be an investment. I just thought you might be interested, that's all. You know, getting architects, planning permission, all that kind of thing. I'll agree a fair price with you. Plus a management fee for running the property after the conversion."

There's an awkward silence. Shane can sense the business potential and, after all, it's hardly a landmark building.

"We'd be partners, in a sense, would we, Jack?"

I hesitate for a moment, not certain quite what he means.

"Well, we'd certainly be colleagues, Shane."

He laughs. Not exactly a friendly laugh.

"Well, that would be fun for both of us, wouldn't it, Jack?"

"Could be, Shane."

Silence.

"OK, it's probably a good business deal. I didn't realize you'd taken so much in about the place. Such a short visit . . . But maybe you went for a walk last night before you went to bed?"

He knows everything. Probably even knows the girl, Deirdre. What the hell? We're all grown up and I've got what I want. And he can help me keep it. And I'm not talking about the girl.

"So, that's settled then? You'll send me plans, cost estimates, including your own, Shane? We'll keep in close contact."

"Will you come back yourself to see how it's going?"

"No, I won't. I'll rely on you, Shane, and I'll send someone over regularly from De Groot Collis. I've complete confidence in you running the whole enterprise."

"Well now, Jack, I take that as a compliment."

"That's how it's meant, Shane."

There's a silence. Which of us should finish this conversation, I wonder?

"OK, Jack," he says. "Leave it with me. I'll start making enquiries right away. I'll ring you next week, if not before. Goodbye, Jack. I'm glad I made that phone-call to you a couple of days ago. Could turn out to be the most lucrative call of my life. And to think I nearly didn't do it! Isn't Fate an amazing thing, Jack?"

"It is indeed, Shane."

"OK, I'll send an outline of an agreement. We'll need the lawyers, I'm afraid. Just so everything's crystal-clear. We don't want anything to muddy the waters, do we now?"

"Absolutely not."

Finishing this conversation is taking longer than I thought. I remain silent and finally he's off the phone.

Soon the Malamore of my childhood, the internal landscape of the house, will be destroyed and with it the catalyst to devastating memory. A memory which could pull down around me the construction within which Kate has for so long been protected. My heart is beating slightly faster than normal. It's an unpleasant sensation. I've nothing more this afternoon other than preparation for my hospital sessions tomorrow. I'll do that later.

I shock Mrs. Jones by saying, "I'm going to my bedroom for an hour or two."

To help me relax I switch on the television. There's an old black-and-white movie on, *Kind Hearts and Coronets*. I fall asleep to the lethally dulcet tones of Joan Greenwood's Sybilla as she explains to D'Ascoyne why she *can't possibly marry him because he's too poor*.

By the time I wake up, it's the seven o'clock news. The exuberance of Jon Snow's tie is in terrible contrast to the litany of catastrophe: famine, Africa; incompetence, Britain; intransigence, Ireland; arrogance, France; overweening smugness, America; ending with an anti-elitist diatribe from a government minister ably supported by a twenty-something ladette. I feel, apart from the insights from the ladette, that I've been listening to the same news for the last twenty years.

I'm still tired, even after my rest. And I haven't even

begun the most important meeting of the day. I decide to have a bath and change for my encounter. After scrambled eggs and toast, I spend an hour or two in my study going through my notes for tomorrow. And then I set out early to walk to Eaton Square.

Twenty-two

"What happened to your father?"

Telling Harold has proved easier than I'd thought. He'd greeted me with genuine friendliness and we'd gone immediately to his study.

He'd poured each of us a brandy and said, "Right. I'm glad you've asked to see me, Jack. You'd be surprised at how much I've guessed. Of course, I could have investigated, sorry . . . that's not the right word, but you know what I mean . . . Did you know that your ex-mother-in-law was, in her youth, a great friend of both my father and my uncle?"

We'd looked at each other.

"Yes, so I believe."

"It was a surprise to me – this connection," he continues. "It's amazing, isn't it, how they still seek to protect us, even when we're adults?"

"Yes."

"Jack, I want to start out with Kate in the very best possible way. Kate's my last chance. That's how I see it. I want the prize. What you've just told me has helped me enormously. It makes me confident that I can make her happy. Does that sound arrogant?"

"No. And I wouldn't be here, Harold, if I didn't feel confident that you'll be very good for her."

I'd told him in concise, formal sentences, the structure of which he no doubt attributed to grief, of our mother's death; its violent, though I believed accidental, nature; the terrible, sudden dispossession of two children of all that they had previously taken for granted. The agonizing time after our father left, when we'd sat alone and silent in the hall, waiting. The imposed exile, the irrevocable decision taken by Edmund never to discuss the past. In short, I'd told Harold the story. He'd said nothing for a while. And then he'd asked what had happened to our father.

"He got six years for manslaughter, and served four," I'd told him.

"Clearly the jury didn't believe it was an accident."

"No."

"But you still believe it."

"Yes."

"He must be an extraordinary man to have elicited such extreme loyalty in such terrible circumstances."

"I think he is."

"Even though he left you and Kate alone in that house . . . after . . . wards . . . ?"

He can't bring himself to say "after he'd shot your mother".

I pause. Finally, I am only able to say, "Yes."

"I've something to confess to you, Jack. I almost thought of buying that house for Kate as a wedding present, for holidays, you know. Mala . . ."

". . . Malamore."

I speak the name of the house as though I genuinely want to help him. And even though I trust him, it's only up to a point. It's not beyond the bounds of possibility that at some time in the future, he might persuade himself to try his own prescription for handling traumatic history. (It takes years to feel certain of survival. That dangerous certainty is sometimes followed by potentially fatal psychological hubris.) Should such a thing happen to Kate, I have now ensured that Malamore will bear no resemblance to the house of Kate's memory.

Also, I've given him the script for intimate conversation concerning the past, which couples believe essential to a long relationship. I've given Harold a history, one which he can guard for Kate. But I have denied him the possibility to extemporize.

"Kate's never recovered, has she?"

"No, in a sense she hasn't."

"She's never seen a psychiatrist?"

"No."

"Why not? You, of all people, must have considered . . ."

"I considered it. Yes. But Edmund, on the single occasion it was mentioned, was vehemently opposed and, eventually, so was Kate. Personally, I think she's done rather well." I deliberately sound slightly defensive and it's not a total lie. She has survived. That's quite an achievement.

He rushes in. "She's remarkable in every way. She hasn't allowed it to destroy her life – no doubt due in large part to you."

"I don't think so. Though I hope I've helped. Kate has her own reserves of strength."

We pause for a moment. I'm grateful. This intensity of concentration is exhausting.

"How did they find your father?" he asks.

"He gave himself up eventually. After he'd gone to a friend of his, a priest, to organize things for us. And had spent time with Edmund, discussing our future I would imagine. Though Edmund never told us anything about their conversations. Silence was deemed best – about everything."

And I remember the silence, which had lain like a deep snow over our past. Hiding everything in a white desolation.

"Where is he now?"

"He's in America. He doesn't want to see us."

"Have you ever seen him since you were a boy?"

"Yes, once. Against his wishes, I might add. And only for an hour or so, just after he was released."

"He sounds a harsh man, and a very strange father."

I say nothing.

Harold comes back to the point, "Why are you telling me this now?"

"Because Kate never could, and because I feel you should know."

"You didn't tell Bronfman, though?"

"No. He couldn't have handled it."

"And I can?"

"Yes. I think you can."

He gets up and walks to the window. He stands with his back to me, an almost Magritte-like figure, framed by the rustling silk curtains, which, undrawn, allow the play of black night and street-lamp to create a momentary reflection in glass.

He turns suddenly towards me and speaks with an insistent intensity, "I know I can. What's more, I know I want to do this – more than anything I have ever wanted to do in my life."

It's uncharted territory, rarely investigated, that strange instinct to a kind of self-immolation which some people inspire in others. It's not gender-based, nor driven by lust or love. Perhaps it lies in dreams of our own past or in an hypothesized image of the other's past. Whatever it is, it's an incitement to — "Now, and for her; or for him". And now is Harold's moment.

I want to say I'm glad, but it seems weak. I remain silent, and this time the silence is comfortable between us.

"Has that secret been the bond between you?" he says at last.

"Yes."

"Who else knows?"

"No one, at least not in this country. And in Ireland, most people have forgotten. It's a long time ago."

"And of course, your names were changed . . ."

"Yes."

"Strange. Kate Trainor doesn't suit her. Harrington suits her much better. And you too, I think, Jack. Do you think Jack Trainor is a kind of *alter ego*? A kind of *doppelgänger*?"

"I don't think so."

I smile at him. I do not say that outside the realms of popular fiction, the *doppelgänger* – that mirror image of the viewer just beyond arm's reach, transparent or, if colour is observed, monochromatic, with only the face or head and trunk "seen" – is mostly experienced by those suffering severe brain injury or cerebral thrombosis. And I don't tell Harold that the Jack Trainor I see whenever I wish to look, which is rarely, is a fourteen-year-old boy, sitting quite still and silent on a wooden chair in a stone hallway, gazing with fervent concentration at the face of his sister.

"Jack, I want to agree something with you. Will you give me a chance now? I can look after her better than you can imagine. But I need to know she's mine. Do you understand?"

He needs to be master now, in order to surrender. It's natural enough.

We look at each other. Sometimes we are caught in a web of femaleness, but there is also a bond that works between men. It is less powerful but has its own grace. We don't shake hands. In silence he sees me to the door.

I walk from Eaton Square to Harley Street. It makes the journey seem longer.

Twenty-three

—

WHEN I get home, she rings me.
"What happened?"
The phrase resonates. But this time she's talking about my conversation with Harold. He'd been embarrassed to admit he'd told Kate of my planned visit to Eaton Square. "Best that it should come from you, Harold," I'd said. The dynamics have changed. As they must.

"He loves you, Kate. He's going to be good for you. You deserve it."

"Why do I feel its all ending"?

I know what she's talking about. I sense in her voice that she is now caught in the loop of hope, which is as contagious as despair. I, too, have taken a careful bet on the future. Fundamental to which was the historical perspective I had, this evening, painted for Harold. The story, which will guide him to certain strengths from his own repertoire, which will make him more beloved by her.

He's the kind of man who needs a cause. He's a kind of urban minotaur, of an age to know this is his last chance and he mustn't blow it. He needs to feel himself worthy at last. He sensed the possibility of a crusade when he ruthlessly left his previous fiancée for Kate. It's part of the root system from which he came, as my father would put it. It's hidden now under layers of worldly success but it's what feeds him still.

We chat on about simple insubstantial things. A normal conversation. So suddenly.

When it's over, and for the first time in many years, I open a locked drawer in my desk and take out a faded newspaper cutting. The yellowed portrait of my father falls, as though decapitated, on to my desk. I look down at it and read the caption:

"Amongst the men released from prison today was . . ."

And they printed my father's name, cold on the page, in a short column from a local paper. It's a shabby-looking souvenir. But I handle the narrow little piece of newsprint as though it were a priceless antique.

That day rushes back to me, gathering sound and speed unrelentingly like the train had seemed to, when I'd first glimpsed it miles down the track. That day, a Friday, when I had gone to meet him at the station.

Edmund, I'd found out later, had had to insist that my father should see me at least once before he left to begin a new life in America. Exactly where in America had not been specified.

I was eighteen and it was my last summer as a school-boy, an English public school boy. Edmund had adopted us formally and we'd taken his name, which probably added to the illusion that London had always been home. To regard myself as English seemed natural to me at the time and indeed still does.

Just as some totally English *grande dame* will casually tell you, "Actually, I was born in India, spent the first eight years of my life there" – without any intimation that this should have had any greater effect on her sense of nationality than if she'd said, "I was born on the south coast, you know, near Worthing" – I too reply, when asked, "In fact I was born in Ireland. I spent the first fourteen years of my life there." And I have no instinct that this undermines my elected definition of my nationality. Mostly the response is, "God, I love the Irish. They're so *friendly*." A response that never seemed to change even when the IRA bombed English shopping malls, barracks and businesses, and murdered men, women and children. "Marvellous people, the Irish. I adore them, they're just so *warm*," and I say, "I suppose so. I haven't been there since I was a child." And they say, "Oh, you *must* go back. You *really* must."

I remember the shock of seeing my father that day as he got off the train. Nothing in his face or walk seemed broken or sad or even older. I know now, of course, that age works in its own secret way. Sometimes it lies in wait and then ambushes the unwary. Other times it scrawls through years of dry nights a little tracery of fine lines across the face of the well-known beauty. As though a cartographer wanted to give some guidance to her for the journey.

Time had done little to my father. He'd retained the lazy man's extra quota. As though, not having used it much, time had left him with a deposit in the bank, to be called on later.

He'd taken charge immediately.

"Let's wait in that elegant station café, shall we? They probably haven't painted it in years and we can enjoy that brilliant county-council green that I used to love when I was a child."

He'd walked ahead of me. He hadn't even shaken hands with me, and hugging was out of the question. We'd sat opposite each other and he'd ordered tea and sandwiches.

"I don't have to tell you that I didn't want this meeting. But Edmund insisted. He's asked me for nothing and done a lot, so I couldn't refuse."

His massive understatement of Edmund's enduring kindness seemed lost on him. He continued in an almost businesslike tone,

"Now, you can see I'm well. And Edmund's clever management of the money from the sale means that you're both secure and I have enough to survive perfectly adequately. I'm going to America. Did he tell you that?"

"Yes."

"Did he tell you I'm thinking of getting married again?"

"What?"

"Oh yes. A marvellous young American woman, a lawyer. She's pulled a lot of strings to get me in. As you can imagine, some people might not regard me as the ideal immigrant . . ."

We looked at each other.

"So, Lawyer Lee, as I call her, is a godsend in a way. Though my belief in the Almighty is more fragile than it used to be."

"America's a long way away." I sounded bleak.

"Yes."

"But it's so far."

"America's the place for me." The note was firm.

There was silence for a minute.

"How did you meet her?"

"Lady visitors, you know, to the lads! She moved on from fascination with a young man, a handsome poet who wanted to die for the cause but instead sent two of his neighbours to their Maker, to me, the older man with a proven passionate nature. Never underestimate a woman's desire to save a man, to release him from his prison, if you like."

He must have suddenly felt sorry for me, his son, the vanquished one. The one who seemed stunned into silence by the mythical power of the father, whom men see as the source of who they are, because he'd softened his tone and had said:

"I returned the letters, yours and Kate's, for a reason. Forgetfulness is possible. Revisiting old scenes doesn't change what happened in them. You know the play's the same no matter how many actors play the part. Come to that, no matter how many audiences see it. I did a bit of acting in . . . well, it passed the time."

"Don't you want to ask me what I'm going to do with my life?"

"No. I know, looking at you, that you'll be fine."

"How?"

I needed to know – as though he had magical powers.

"Oh, I just know."

I'd felt ridiculously reassured. That fabricated power again.

"And don't you want to ask me about Kate?"

He'd paused and had drunk slowly from the cracked cream cup, which seemed to nest, hidden in his large hands.

"Ah, well, Kate . . . What Kate needs, and what Kate will always need, is the kind of man who will lift her up high above reality, so that it's blurred when she looks down. Now we understand that, don't we, Jack? We have a pact. Isn't that right?"

And I remembered blinking furiously, my eyes flickering at manic speed at the implication of all that I knew and of all that was ahead of me. The study, the obsessive attention to expression, whether vocal or physical, terrified of missing something vital that might destroy everything.

"I want to go now, Jack. I'm sorry. Talking does no good. The facts can't be changed."

"But I need to talk to you. I want to talk to you."

"I'd talk to you from now till the day I die if I thought it wouldn't kill you. You've got to know the thing is dead, over. And talking just keeps it alive. You've got to starve the bastard, otherwise it just grows and grows until all you are, is whatever cursed thing felled you."

"And Mother?"

"Mother! Mother?" He almost whispered it. "Is that what you call her now? Mother. Hmm. Catherine would be surprised. You know we didn't start out to be mother or father. The most natural thing in the world, they say. I wonder? It's an awful trick Nature plays on us to get us to take up the roles. And I'm not talking about avoidance tactics and all the breakthroughs they've made now. No, there's something else afoot. Always has been. We started out Catherine and Michael . . . and then . . . and then . . . Right, enough of this. I'm going now."

He'd stood up. My father. A man defined beyond the boundaries of character, ethics, fame or wealth. My father. The source of all I am. He'd waved me away and had walked towards the steps to the bridge, which led to the platform opposite me. A train had then obscured him. I had sat down again and had tried, unsuccessfully, not to cry.

This memory leads to such an all-consuming state of agitation that the physical power of it virtually propels me out of my chair. I begin to walk frantically round the room as though in its corners I might find some comfort. But this time my beloved house cannot calm me.

Memory and the newspaper cutting, that scroll of dead times, defeat us both.

I'm almost hysterically tired, but I ring him anyway. It's an emergency-only number, which he updates by post with strict instructions to use it only *in extremis*.

"Father?"

"Well, that can only be you. Only one man in the world can call me that."

And there it is again. That slow voice, *basso profundo*, even when not contrasted, as it usually is in my memory, with hers, that light, quick scurrying note – up the scale most often. I am immediately calmed. A lot can happen between people without anything changing. Even after all these years, he has the same gift to soothe. Or is it that it's easier to love the father, believing him less culpable for our existence?

"I just needed to ring you tonight. I think it's all coming to an end. I think she's definitely . . . saved? Is that the word I'm looking for?"

"Could be. Though any word will do as long as you're sure. Are you sure?"

"As sure as one ever can be. She's going to get married again. I've taken a calculated risk and given him a version of events. He can use that as . . ."

". . . Her history?"

"Everyone needs one. One they can live with."

"What makes you think he's going to tell it right?"

"He's got a history of his own. He's a reconstructionist. They're all over London, the children of immigrants given a *tabula rasa* on which to write their story. Though they don't see themselves like that, of course. Second generation from a generation that taught itself survival. Good instincts."

"The roots go deep." He sounds as though he's repeating a mantra.

"So you always said."

"You'd have grown bored with me, Jack, if you'd had the time. But you never had that chance. Hell of a thing to lose out on – growing bored with your parents."

"You should have done my job."

"Me? Sure, I did nothing. I was a very lazy man, Jack, you know that. At least you must remember that she never minded."

"Left you more time for her . . ."

"Ah, that's mean, Jack. That's mean. Anyway, if you read your literature, Jack, the great love affairs – they're virtually a full-time job."

He laughs. He's a happy man. It's a mysterious gift, like a talent for music perhaps. Does it require practice, I wonder?

"That's why there are so few great love affairs any more. At least, looking round, I don't see many."

I want to ask him about the woman he's with. I don't even know if it's the same one. But I can't. I'm frightened I could lose this moment with him. I'm cautious, the way those who've lost are cautious. They know it can happen.

"He's older, adores her, of course."

"Lack of adoration has never been her problem. It's a power they have to make us feel there's something spiritually good in our adoration of them."

"And when it's the other way round?"

"You're asking me? I thought you were the expert, Jack."

"Mostly from reading. And, of course, watching you two, over and over in my mind."

"Ah well, it's time to stop that now. Don't you think?

It's your chance now, in a way, to be free . . . I think we've gone far enough. Think we should finish now."

"Father . . ."

"I know the things you want to say. But don't. It was my responsibility in the end. I've been thinking about it for years. Read a bit, you know. Poetry, classics. Brian Connolly would be proud of me . . ."

I want to tell him about the letter, but he's talking about my mother. I daren't miss a word.

"She lived high up on some other plain, in a kind of passionate dream of me. The smallest thing threatened the giddy high-wire act of Catherine and Michael. She wanted it seamless. As though we'd been knitted into one another. Even a single loose thread was a prophecy of unravelment to her. I let her fall. I wasn't careful enough. The rest is a technicality. It's a heavy burden, a woman's adoration. Anyway, it's to be feared. With good cause, in my case. You've carried this a long time, Jack. I'm grateful. Well . . . goodbye now."

And he put the phone down.

We are like old soldiers who can only refer in passing to the experience which made our lives. And even then, only rarely, every ten or twenty years or so. And there are rules to the conversation. They're from an old almanac, which teaches that some things should not be articulated. Words, when released, fly sometimes like predatory birds towards their victim. What is not spoken can be dealt with in silence and in the dark.

I sit here in these rooms every day and I listen to words. Sometimes I feel as though I see them; the sound-painted pictures of a human life. Which, of course, they're not. What I hear and see is the event-altered perspective of the entire experience. Is it possible that repetition makes individuals blind and deaf to the very thing that might save them?

I feel compelled to look at the date in order to mark this evening in my life. I remember that it's twenty-five years since my mother died. She's been dead now for a quarter of a century, as an historian would put it. It's a long time, either way.

It's time, as my father said, to finish it.

I will now lose Kate. I must now lose her. I must let her go – which is just another way of saying it. She is the love of my life. She is my great love affair. Though not in the sense the words usually mean.

Was I lost for ever that afternoon when we were asked to reconstruct the event? Did the vision of her, so young, so small, so indefatigable, colour-wash my mind indelibly? Is that why other visions seem so vapid in comparison? Or, is it that to watch her cheat the shadows with such careful grace just takes my breath away?

What is available to other women in my life is a certain expert sexuality and shallow sighs at the heart's interminable frustrations. The well-known signs of pleasant, though little, loves.

The great thing is over.

Kate and I will no longer dance. She will not ask me. She too has sensed her own survival. How strange that I never felt a single spark of desire for her, not even when we danced naked together.

No, that was a communion. A ritual to celebrate the moving tableau which was our last vision of them, our utterly beautiful parents, naked, dancing, not in their bedroom but in the attic where new guns, and old treasures, were carefully locked away. The forbidden place, to which we had followed them, ambivalently, excitedly, secretly. Looking for the answer to the mystery of parental love. A fatal quest, as I learned young and relearn weekly in my consulting rooms. Not all of us are lost parents but most of us are, at some time, lost children.

Is it our first creative act, the myth of our immaculate conception, in which for a time parents collude? And is our first great act of destruction due to fury that we were not the sole purpose of their being together? Since every generation seems to play out this story, perhaps it is essential to the human in us.

Except that for Kate and me, it's more complicated. We have different versions of the story. They have run parallel for most of our lives.

In Kate's version, her father was found guilty of the manslaughter of her mother. It was not murder, though a doubt took root and remains in her mind. That burden is heavy enough for anyone to carry and I think she's done wonderfully. I really do. But it's been very hard. Once or twice I feared that she wouldn't just stumble – which I could handle – but that she would fall so badly she would shatter. And if that had happened, I might never have been able to put her back together again. She might have been beyond reconstruction. As it is, her life has been a series of mini-deaths and resurrections.

I think my mother, if she saw Kate now, would be pleased. In fact, I'm sure she would. Though how can I ever know?

She was laughing, wildly, on that long-ago Sunday in August when we'd crept unseen into the attic and hidden behind an old chest of drawers, from which yards of worn-out curtains tumbled. Peeping out carefully from either side, we'd gazed, almost hypnotized, at our ecstatic parents as they danced together in perfect time, though there was no music. Her head was thrown back, and his face, its expression puzzled, was bent over hers as though in her eyes he would find the answer to some vital question. There was something sculptural about their dense, white nakedness as for a second the dancing stopped.

Suddenly, from nowhere, that fatal ferocity, which like shrieking birds seemed always to hover round her, erupted, as she beat him with her fists, pounding him round his heart, crying:

"Oh, Michael, I will kill you, I will truly kill you if you ever, ever touch . . ."

And then, our world exploded and burned out. What is noted in the moment of conflagration remains indelible. Though not everything is noted. A sensation of emotional vertigo does not allow for precision as layers of presumed reality collapse, the way trembling buildings do in an earthquake. But of this I'm certain. Her face as she fell dead to the floor, did not look frightened. Nor did it wear that surprised look which is a Hollywood staple and which has entered the pictorial archive of our mind. She was all mother as she fell, in a way that perhaps she'd never been before. That's what I think anyway.

But he knew her best. In the terrible second in which she went spinning out of his life, he must have seen the horror in her face at what would become of their precious daughter. After all, he was not just her lover, who did his utmost to contain the absolute, violent passion that she felt for him. He also played father to her own particular version of mother. A role, to which even she knew she was not best suited. Nature had designed her for an extreme of sexual love, the force of which disoriented them both and fatally dulled parental vision. Such appalling love leaves us aghast and, sometimes, stricken with envy.

There is not a day I do not hope that in her last seconds she saw it all and sensed how sublime he would be. Yes, that's the word. He was sublime. In a split second he lifted from Kate the burden of her guilt, a primitive guilt which is, and always has been, unendurable. He wrenched it from her and carried it away. It requires supernatural strength, as when a parent lifts the car under which his child is trapped, or struggles on against the odds to alert the rescue team. We need those tales when we're young and it may be demanded of us to act them out, when we are older.

That day, in my father's case what was required was another form of salvation. He did not cry out as his wife slipped from his arms but as though a primitive impulsion drove him, turned and threw himself headlong across Kate, who stood there, paralysed. He took the gun, seeming to wipe it from her hand, as though it were a stain. Then, as his huge body blocked Kate's vision, with studied precision he fired over the body of his dead wife.

In that strange state, which follows trauma and which destroys or suspends human responsiveness, we remained silent and becalmed. Like painted figures in a painted room. Then our father, having pulled an old piece of material – of a kind of faded gold colour – round him, placed an outstretched hand on our heads like a benediction, and turning us round, guided us from the room. As we passed the chair on which his clothes were neatly folded, he told me to pick them up. Then he carefully lifted the now starkly frozen Kate and I silently followed as he carried her to the bathroom. Dazed, I stood to one side as he washed her Coppelia-like figure and wrapped her in a towel. Under orders again, I too washed myself. And as though in a dream I listened to him as he whispered to her over and over that poor Daddy had done a terrible thing, that there had been the most dreadful accident and that maybe Daddy would have to go away.

Then he took me to my room and told me to change my clothes while he went with Kate to her bedroom. When he came back, holding Kate by the hand, I saw that he had her stained Sunday dress over his arm. He motioned to me to give him my own clothes, which I'd thrown on the floor. We then silently walked with him up the casement staircase to our parents' bedroom.

He dressed hurriedly in this now strange room, and with Kate sitting silently outside, he shaped the moment for me. He scooped up words from somewhere. It seemed to me then, and still does, that it was a tangible thing he handed to me that day. Dense and heavy, like a statue carved from stone.

Afterwards, he sat us opposite each other in the stone hallway and rehearsed us in the reconstruction of the event.

We heard him move round the house, and heard the keys turn in many doors. He took our watches from us, and with a kind of smile, kissed them and put each one carefully into a different pocket. Then he left us, locking the back door behind him, prisoners in our own house, longing for our jailer.

And we did as we were told and repeated the reconstruction over and over to each other, until the men came and, sitting beside us, asked us to tell them in our own words . . .

The infliction of innocence requires the assumption of

guilt. His essential, much condemned desertion of us afterwards, would, he believed, prove him guilty. He was right. His reward? Well, he gave his daughter a just about adequate life. There was a price. She was robbed of a brutal truth; the reason was love. Only occasionally do I ask myself, is love a good enough reason? And my reward? I helped. He knew that would save me too. I had a job to do and, honestly, fourteen is not all that young to start.

Twenty-four

—

TOMORROW . . . TOMORROW? That net of time which trawls us on and on, towards . . . Well, in this case, towards Thursday. Thursday, which, as it's now well after midnight, is in a sense already here. A hospital day. A heavy day. It's always a heavy day at the hospital.

I remember that I didn't check my surgery answer machine before I left for Eaton Square. Though it's nearly two a.m. I press the button. Patrick Dufors . . .

"Sorry, I know it's late. He's just died. I told him. I sat beside him and I told him. The thing is, I'm not certain . . . but I don't think he heard a word. But I can't be sure. I'll never know, really . . . Till Monday then . . ."

I close my eyes.

Brenda's voice . . . "Marion Masters has cancelled her next appointment. She didn't give a reason."

Oh, God.

I turn off the lights and sit for a few moments in the semi-darkness. I should try to get some sleep. I owe it to my patients. They are sleeping now – and will wake to the certainty of my arrival, to the absolute certainty that I will listen. To the possibility that I may even help.

Idly, I press my private answer machine on my way to the door.

Cora. She's in seductive mood. Honeyed tones. I sigh, but reluctantly I'm drawn to all that sweetness.

"Jack, it's late and I just wanted to say I had a very

217

happy time last Sunday. Just that. I felt I really had to say thank you. And Jack . . . I love you. I truly love you."

That girl makes me smile. She's got me in her sights. She's going to take me over. Perhaps this time, like Barkis, I'm willing. For reasons she will never understand.

I can almost hear her in a year or so, telling friends how "difficult" I was, in the beginning. Which will, of course, underline how clever she was to "get me". How one day it just . . . "seemed right". I'll smile of course and give that rueful look the male has perfected when faced with inevitable surrender. Hell, I'll probably enjoy it.

I'll delete Poppy Bright's number. Now. Why not? It's a start. Isn't it?

But tonight, before I sleep, I'll play that reel of memory just one more time before I finally erase it. Just once more . . .

Then I'm swimming to the surface and this time I'm going to stay there.